T0208094

The Stockton Saga 4

The Stockton Saga 4

The Lady From Colorado

Steven Douglas Glover

THE STOCKTON SAGA 4
THE LADY FROM COLORADO

iUniverse books may be ordered through booksellers or by contacting:

iUniverse
1663 Liberty Drive
Bloomington, IN 47403
www.iuniverse.com
1-800-Authors (1-800-288-4677)

ISBN: 978-1-4917-8122-7 (sc)
ISBN: 978-1-4917-8123-4 (e)

Print information available on the last page.

iUniverse rev. date: 10/26/2015

CONTENTS

PREFACE

The *Stockton Saga* began as a short story for a friend. Her positive response encouraged me to write yet another tale of adventure. As others read my stories of gunfighter, Cole Stockton, suggestions were made to put them together as a novel. Thus, *The Stockton Saga: Dawn of the Gunfighter* was born. It chronicles his heritage and the elements that formed his mystique.

The stories of Cole Stockton, a man of strong moral character, are countless. *The Stockton Saga 2: Star of Justice* followed, revealing Stockton's rise to Deputy U.S. Marshal as well as meeting his ladylove, Laura Sumner. My bounty of narratives about this man of the law led to *The Stockton Saga 3: A Man to Reckon With*. It continues Cole's encounters in the Lower Colorado Territory during the last half of the 19th century.

I thought it time to highlight the women of the Old West. This book, *The Stockton Saga 4: The Lady From Colorado*, presents lady rancher Laura Sumner in several situations that reveal her strength of character. She encounters danger on several occasions, oversees wranglers as she works alongside them on her horse ranch and fights for justice for her aging parents. U. S. Marshal Cole Stockton remains a principle character in the novel.

I try to portray the Old West as it actually was, lending authenticity to the stories. Historical characters have been researched. When I speak of certain weapons, pistol or rifle, they have been researched as well. Smallest details of life and times, currency, fashion, food, furniture, businesses, are each presented as they were in the latter half of the 19th century. My accounts are fiction and written for enjoyment. They are not intended to be historically accurate by specific date, incident or actual person.

Immeasurable appreciation goes to my dear friend, Monti Lynne Eastin for the persona of Laura Sumner. Her support of my writing and continuous prompting me to publish them is genuinely appreciated.

Immense gratitude is given to Gay Lynn Auld for her time and effort editing this manuscript. Her suggestions for expansion proved invaluable.

A special thanks to Linda Glover, without whose review and moral support this book would not have been published.

A very special thanks to my dedicated fans who continue to read my books and request more.

I humbly dedicate this book to my special friend of many years.
This one is for you,

Monti Lynne Eastin

and

To the memory of

Louis L'amour
1908 - 1988

CHAPTER ONE

Reflection

On a rare occasion when the daylight outlasted the list of chores at the Sumner Horse Ranch in the lower Colorado Territory, Laura Sumner, owner and Boss Wrangler, took stock of her life. The day's chores were already done and her wranglers were relaxing in the bunkhouse from the previous two weeks of breaking the latest catch of wild horses to saddle stock. These newly trained mounts would be sold to miners, cattlemen, and others around the area.

A soft breeze wafted strands of dark hair across Laura's face as she sat on the porch of the ranch house. The young woman carefully placed her mug of freshly brewed coffee on an old wooden table nearby, then brushed the hair from her tanned face.

Momentarily, she stood, took a deep breath of fresh mountain air, stretched a bit, then surveyed the blazing sunset of the lower Colorado Territory. The rustle of trees brought a covey of quail to flight. The boss lady heard faint voices from the bunkhouse as her boys played checkers, cards, and swapped stories with each other. The soft strumming of a guitar brought a smile to her face. Voices joined in soft harmony with the instrumentalist as a favorite ballad played. This was her domain, the Sumner Horse Ranch, the LS Ranch.

Laura sank into the wooden rocker, took a sip of the fresh brew and closed her eyes. Within moments, she was ten again, home on the family farm between Dallas and Fort Worth.

She was tending her very own garden. The harvest was her victory. Tears swelled when she thought of her parents, Carroll and Mary, so far away in Texas, yet so close in her heart. Reflecting on their struggle to clear the land and till the soil on their homestead, Laura found every day a deeper understanding of their sacrifices and appreciation for her rearing.

Her parents loved the land and passed that love on to their only child. Now, as a landowner in the wilds of the Colorado Territory, she perpetuated their frontier spirit.

Laura recalled meeting her father's older brother Uncle Jesse when he came to visit. It was Uncle Jesse who instilled the love of horses in Laura. This growing love of horses changed Laura's life, and brought her to Colorado.

Recalling her first visit to Uncle Jesse in the Colorado Territory, Laura brought memories of the stagecoach holdup, the murder of a fellow passenger, and unexpected manner of six-gun justice to those that held them up.

On that first visit, Laura found that she loved the clean air of the Rocky Mountains and the sweet scent of wildflowers drifting on soft breezes across the meadows.

The excitement of riding along with her uncle and his wranglers on their horse hunting expeditions remained in her memory. She found mountain thunderstorms exhilarating. To Laura, there was nothing quite like the smell of the land after a fresh rain.

Laura learned all she could from Uncle Jesse about catching wild horses, taming them, and selling them to various mining operations, local cattle ranchers, other folks that needed good horseflesh in their daily business, and especially the army that needed frequent remounts. Under Jesse's guidance, Laura became a superb horsewoman and quite versed with a six-gun and Winchester rifle.

Laura found new excitement on her return to her parents' farm in Texas. She found the affection of a suitor. To her heartbreak, this experience turned sour when she found him in the arms of another.

Immediately after the relationship failed, Laura received a letter from a lawyer in the Colorado Territory relating that Uncle Jesse had been murdered. Unexpectedly, her uncle had willed his horse ranch holdings to her. Although devastated by his loss, the young woman resolved to seek out her destiny in Colorado, as Uncle Jesse obviously wished her to.

Laura breathed deeply, exhaling softly. In the next instant, she relived her first encounter with Cole Stockton, a gunfighter turned Deputy U.S. Marshal. He became her best friend, confidant, and true love. Cole taught Laura further in the use of firearms. Now, she was as good or better than most men with either revolver or rifle.

Laura fondly remembered the prophetic words of an elderly woman back home, known for telling fortunes. Maude Pritchard told Laura in reading her tea leaves, "You love horses. You have been to the mountains and seen your destiny." Maude continued, "One will stoke the fires of your soul. He is born of deadly skill, yet you will seek the comfort of his honor." Laura smiled as she thought of the tender moments that she and Cole shared.

In challenging times as a fledging rancher, it was Cole, who sent the most trusted wranglers to her. Now, Judd Ellison, one of the first men, was her foreman and mentor on the LS Ranch.

Judd had become her ranching business mainstay. He knew horses, and he knew men. With Judd's guidance, the LS Ranch had the best of wranglers and the best of methods to deliver horses to customers. Working together, the ranch gained the enviable reputation of having the finest trained horses in the territory.

Although born and raised in Texas, Laura had become a woman of the Territory. Colorado was now her home, and it felt good to her. Perhaps statehood would come soon.

In quiet moments like this one on the porch at twilight, from the back of her mind came the nagging thought, "Why did Uncle Jesse will this ranch to me? Why did he not will this ranch to his only child?" Laura couldn't know it then, but her question would soon have an answer.

Within a matter of days, a situation would unfold in the small town of Miller's Station, Colorado Territory. This event would remove any doubt, and confirm why Uncle Jesse had chosen to correctly to leave his Colorado holdings to Laura.

* *

Joel Martin owned the general store that included a post office at Miller's Station near the passes of the Lower Colorado. He enjoyed the postal part of his business because he learned firsthand the excitement in the lives of the people of the community from their mail. Joel often daydreamed about the places postmarked on the letters he delivered to folks. He promised himself that someday, he would visit some of them.

This particular morning, he picked up a letter addressed to Laura Sumner. It was postmarked New York City. Who would post a letter to Laura from New York City? She was a Texas girl. His mind played games with him. Was she planning to leave the Territory? What was her connection to the East? What would Cole Stockton think?

Laura was a woman of the West, and conducted herself as such— she could ride, and ride well. She wrangled horses better than most men, and could even shoot better than most men. Of course, Laura had the best mentor, namely, Cole Stockton. He was a known gunfighter and presently the Deputy U.S. Marshal assigned to the Territory of the Lower Colorado.

Joel took a second look at the letter. The return address read *Victoria Stinson*. The curious postmaster spoke the name aloud, "Victoria." The name rang of Eastern society.

As a stroke of coincidence, Joel looked up to see Laura Sumner dismount her black horse Mickey in front of his general store. She spoke briefly to a few of the older citizens who sat in their favorite chairs on the porch, then ambled on in to the store, glancing over various displays of merchandise.

Laura approached Joel with a pleasant smile. "Good morning, Joel. Would there be any mail for us folks at the LS Ranch?" Joel smiled back in response as he handed her the letter from the East.

Laura glanced at the return address with a puzzled expression, then slowly opened the letter. Reading intently, her eyes widened with a look of great surprise. Joel was about to inquire about the letter, when Laura spun on her heel. She dashed out the door with a quick "Thank you, Joel," and mounted Mickey. Turning toward the end of town, they disappeared in a whirlwind cloud of dust.

Three quarters of an hour later, Laura Sumner rode into her ranch yard, calling out for her foreman Judd Ellison.

"Judd—Judd Ellison, where are you? I need to speak with you— now!"

Judd appeared from behind the barn door, "Laura! I'm over here. What is it? What's going on?"

"Judd, we have, rather, I have—a big problem. I'm going to ask a lot from you and the boys for a while. About two weeks' worth, I would say. I know you will not fully understand, but I need your help, and in some most probable strange ways."

"Just name it, boss," replied Judd. He continued, "Me and the boys will do anything for you—you know that. What seems to be the problem?"

Judd studied Laura's face for clues to her dismay. "We'll handle anything that comes your way. What is it, Laura? Is it rustlers? outlaws? Indians? fire? stampede? somebody lost? somebody needs help? We'll do it. What is it, Laura?"

"Worse than ALL that, Judd. My spoiled, wealthy cousin, Victoria, her husband, and their butler, are coming from New York City to spend two weeks at this ranch. I believe that they are already on the road. By the postmark on this letter, they might be here within the coming week. We've got to get this place in tiptop shape—for show, or I'll never live it down. Victoria is the image of social perfection, and I must act like a lady while she is here."

"I see what you mean, Laura. You are not exactly the genteel society type. I don't mind telling you that there's been times that I would've preferred to rope a whirlwind than to disappoint you; however, we— the boys and I—wouldn't have it any other way. What is it that you want us to do?"

"Well, for one, Judd, you've got to act like a gentleman."

"Laura, we boys don't even have the foggiest idea what a gentleman is supposed to be like. I mean, we know some basic manners and such, but we sure don't know how to talk fancy, and dress like dudes. We are just what we are—horse wranglers."

Judd thought for a moment, "If you will give us a talk and teach us some in the next few days, I'm sure that we will all give it our best try."

"That's fair enough, Judd. That reminds me, have you seen Cole Stockton today?"

"Yes, Laura, I did. He rode out early this morning. He said that he had to go to see Judge Wilkerson in Denver. He mentioned that he would be in Denver about a week."

"Oh, great! That's just great! Help me get his things out of the spare room, and move them to a place in the bunkhouse. He just can't be living in the main house—not with Victoria coming. He will just have to understand."

"Laura," reflected Judd, "Cole is and always will be a gentleman. He will understand."

"Yes, Judd. He has always been understanding. But—but, this is different. He's—well, you know how it is with us. I really hope that he will understand."

Chapter Two

The Easterners

Uniformed porters lined the platform as the Union Pacific passenger train from New York City chugged into the station at the sprawling Great Lakes city of Chicago. The powerful steam engine ground its iron wheels in reverse, spinning to a skidding halt. Steam clouds burst from the boiler as the train came to rest along the loading platform.

Passengers in the front cars disembarked and walked toward the station house. They would be changing trains for other destinations, or arranging transportation to different areas of the city. The first class cars to the rear of the train were luxurious, catering to the every whim of the wealthy. Porters assisted each pampered passenger down the small steps to the wooden platform below while others saw to the unloading of luggage from the baggage cars.

Victoria Sumner-Stinson, attired in a stylish deep purple traveling dress, stepped daintily down from the first class coach. Her clear blue eyes shined with excitement. They were on their way Westward. Her flaxen hair was neatly pinned under an exquisite custom creation from Paris. She was the picture of Eastern society.

Victoria turned to watch her husband Walter Stinson, the wealthy founder and owner of *Stinson's Mercantile & Dry Goods*, step down to the boardwalk platform. He was dressed in an immaculate white shirt, silk tie, vest with solid gold watch on a double braided chain, and dark suit. A custom gray Stetson New Yorker completed the attire. With a freshly trimmed dark brown mustache, he cut the perfect image of a gentleman.

Butler Mason Bronfeld wore a smartly tailored dark suit as well, and topped it off with a bowler hat. Mason stepped down to the platform, surveyed the scene, then walked down the line of cars to direct the transfer of luggage to the next train traveling toward Colorado.

Victoria and Walter walked side by side into the large station house where they sought and entered the traveler's lounge. The *Lounge* was known as a haven for the elite of society in a very busy train station. It included a bar as well as comfortable sofas and chairs. They would be there about four hours awaiting the train west.

Victoria entered the Lounge with a stately air about her. She glanced about the room with calculating glance. She passed over a widow dressed in black, a woman with two children, and another woman sitting with four children and a nanny.

There were others she passed over that didn't seem to fit her personality. Finally, Victoria spied three women engaged in conversation around a small table, and there was an empty chair. The ladies were sipping lemonade or iced tea. Victoria decided to introduce herself.

Victoria busied herself visiting with the other ladies, making certain they heard of her destination to a Western horse ranch.

"We are traveling to the Colorado Territory to visit with my cousin, Laura Sumner. Although my cousin was born and raised on a small farm in Texas, she has elevated her status. She now owns a horse ranch in the Rockies. I can just picture it. There are undoubtedly many beautiful horses, sprawling fields of green where we will go riding, picnicking, have extravagant social teas, and a Fourth of July Ball. I know that Laura will introduce me to just everyone who is *anybody* there in the Territory. I have packed two exquisite riding habits and several new frocks. After all, one must look her best when meeting people of means."

The other ladies listened with interest and envy. They bid her safe journey as porters announced train departures, causing each to leave the Lounge.

Walter and Mason passed the time of day with a few gentlemen as they stood at the massive curved bar with a cigar and a brandy. Walter Stinson reached into his inside vest pocket and produced the train tickets. He glanced once more at the details of their next destination. Omaha, Nebraska was the next stop. Walter sighed. He knew nothing of this place and assumed that it would be a place of smelly cattle pens since it was a rail town. He would not have chosen the West for this year's vacation. He preferred to go to Europe.

New Yorkers, having read considerable articles in the newspapers and magazines about the Wild West, considered anywhere west of the Mississippi as less than civilized. They conjured up visions of wild

Indians, difficult stagecoach journeys, crude women, and men who packed guns.

Walter certainly had no intention of leaving the comfort of modern society to travel to a land that lacked refinement. However, Victoria was adamant. They would travel west. Whatever Victoria wanted, Victoria got. Although Walter pondered her motives without conclusion, he did not cross her.

"Just once," thought Walter, "I would like to get the upper hand. I feel threatened by her. I do believe, though, that Victoria wants to see firsthand just what kind of woman that Laura turned out to be, and how imposing her father's horse ranch is to others nearby. After all, it should have been Victoria's inheritance. Why had old man Sumner willed the ranch to Laura, leaving nothing to his own daughter?"

Victoria had no love for her father. When he divorced her mother, he traveled to the West and become one of those *heathens*. Jesse Sumner had turned his back on everything in the East, giving all his possessions to Victoria's mother, and disappeared into the wilds, and from the life of his daughter.

Only recently, Victoria had received a letter from a relative, and learned of Jesse Sumner's fate, and about his Last Will and Testament. Quickly, she decided to correspond with Laura. She would invite Walter and herself to vacation at the Sumner Ranch. Walter thought, "Heaven help us if this Cousin Laura turns out to be more obstinate than Victoria."

* *

The Rock Island Line train ran southwest from Chicago for 494 miles to Omaha. It carried a luxurious Pullman car. The Stinsons relaxed in its comfort while watching the vast prairies pass before their eyes. At each stop westward, however, more and more of the gentlemen and ladies departed the train, and more and more roughly clad frontier settlers boarded.

Soon, the New Yorkers were out of their element. It was difficult to converse with other passengers. There were glances and surprise, undoubtedly at their attire.

Prior to arriving in Omaha, the Stinsons and their butler were the only occupants of the club car. They sat looking at each other, each wondering if they had made the right decision about this trip.

At Omaha, they changed to yet another train, with the next destination Denver. From there, they had to travel the final three days of their journey by stagecoach. Because the Stinsons had never traveled by stagecoach, they had no idea what to expect.

Upon arriving in Denver, they soon learned, much to their disappointment, that the three of them and their baggage were too much for the regularly scheduled coach.

Walter, henceforth, opened his wallet and arranged for a special coach to carry only Victoria, himself, and butler Mason, along with all of their luggage to Miller's Station in the Lower Colorado Territory. Upon arrival, they would contact Laura Sumner for travel to her uncle's horse ranch.

As Walter made travel arrangements, a lone unshaven man stood unobtrusively to the side and listened intently as the agent gave details of the schedule and route of the special coach.

The man furtively spotted the large stack of greenbacks that Walter held in his hand. He appraised the value of Walter's watch, chain, and ring. Here were rich Eastern *softies*, traveling by a special coach, heading toward the wilds. He could not believe his good fortune. This robbery would be easy pickings for him and his two brothers.

Mort Wooley chuckled aloud as he turned and stepped into the street, mounted his horse, and rode out to meet his kinfolk. They would waylay the coach somewhere in the lonely mountainous area, take the money, and live like kings. Mort smiled as he thought of how he would spend his share of the loot.

* *

The Stinsons boarded the special coach. The seats were hard and uncomfortable. This coach had not been used in years, the interior was hot with stale odors and covered with dust.

Victoria drew out her silk handkerchief when she sneezed several times as she inhaled the musty odors. Her eyes watered, and soon turned red rimmed. Walter said nothing about the redness, as he didn't want to contend with her fretting and whining. Mason chuckled to himself.

A grizzled old codger, Sammy Colter, was the only driver available at the time. His shotgun guard turned out to be a young man, barely six months on the job. The coach lurched hard forward as the driver cracked his whip into the air, and cursed a bit, as the six-horse team leaned into their harnesses.

Victoria and Walter collided with the sudden movement. Mason lost his hat as he bolted forward. He methodically rescued it from the floor and filled the coach with dust as he brushed off the bowler.

It took several miles before the three passengers adjusted to their new travel mode. The stifling closeness of the air, dust, and cramped space was like no other travel experience for the trio. Finally, they learned to sway with the movement of the coach, finding it easier to endure the ride.

Throughout the long day, the coach rumbled along at what seemed a slow pace. Going from a sudden thunder storm into a swarm of insects that was followed by a whirlwind, the passengers were so fraught with the elements that they failed to notice the beauty of the pristine countryside.

The coach stopped at numerous way stations allowing the Stinson party the opportunity to step out, stretch their legs, and regain circulation in their limbs. Stagecoach stations were situated so that coaches changed teams at about every twenty-five or thirty miles. Some of these stations offered meals and overnight accommodations for weary passengers. Victoria and Walter could not imagine what spending a night in any of them would consist of.

Victoria despised the food at the way stations; however, she was so hungry that she forced herself to eat the greasy meat, hard biscuits, and unsavory undercooked vegetables. The water, on the other hand, was pleasantly refreshing. Coffee came strong and black, and with sugar added, it resembled sweet mud to Walter and Mason. Victoria refused to drink the nasty brew and wondered if anyone west of the Mississippi River drank hot tea.

The end of the first day's travel found the travelers looking forward to a meal and a room with a comfortable bed. There was none to be had at the stagecoach way station. They settled for two very small rooms with four walls bare, shabby curtains, and a hard mattress each. The passengers were offered a meal of beef and vegetable stew accompanied with sourdough bread and a wild berry cobbler.

Mason's room provided only a single bed, oil lamp on a washstand with pitcher and basin. He neatly folded his suit and shirt and placed them over his valise. Within minutes, he extinguished his lamp and fell into bed.

In their room, the couple prepared for bed quickly with little conversation. Walter was pleased to find a woolen blanket, for the mountain air dropped considerably in temperature during the night. Victoria complained without response from her husband. The small basin and pitcher did not accommodate her nightly beauty routine. The oil in the lamp gave off a black smoke. There were no hangers for her clothes. The chill in the air made her shiver as she undressed. The final straw was the harsh bed linens and rough blanket. Victoria threw the blankets aside and sobbed alone. Walter snored in a dead sleep.

The following morning brought aches and pains from the jostling of the coach the previous day, and a sleepless night. Victoria looked haggard. Dark circles formed under her usually bright blue eyes, which added to her already irritable state.

"Damn," thought Walter. "She is going to be quite unreasonable today, and she looks like hell warmed over."

Breakfast only added to their misery. The room reeked of bacon grease. It was not the best fare they had ever seen. Limp bacon, with potatoes and eggs fried in bacon grease sat in serving platters at the long table in the way station dining room. Greasy eggs cooked sunny side up, with lots of strong, dark coffee greeted them at the long table in the way station.

The men were satisfied with the heavy meal and strong coffee. Biscuits were fresh, with lots of churned butter, and homemade berry jam. Victoria made a meal of the biscuits, butter, and jam. She finished her meal with a glass of buttermilk. Buttermilk made Walter ill, and he turned his head aside to avoid seeing Victoria drinking hers.

At eight o'clock sharp, the stage boarded once again with a fresh six-horse team stretched into the harness to sway and bounce the coach along the well-rutted trail to the Lower Colorado.

Near to ten miles out of the overnight way station, three masked riders dressed in clothes stained with dust and sweat quickly swooped upon the coach. They surrounded it with revolvers drawn. The stagecoach shuddered to a stop, with horses restlessly stomping.

"Guard!" one man yelled, "throw down that there shotgun or get filled with lead. Driver, keep yore hands in plain sight. All right, youse dandies! Drop down out of that coach and surrender your valuables."

Victoria, Walter, and Mason sat shaking with the realization that they were about to be robbed of their valuables. They'd read about such outlaws in the Eastern newspapers. They knew there was nothing they could do about it.

The grizzled old driver, Sammy Colter, turned his head and spit his chaw. He gazed down at the three would-be robbers, and announced, "I sure hope you guys know what you are getting yoreselfs in fer."

"What do you mean?" snapped Zeb Wooley, surprised that the driver would make such a remark.

"Why, boys, we're hauling the Stinson family. The young woman inside the coach is blood kin to Laura Sumner of the Sumner Horse Ranch, and in case that don't strike a note, I'd sure hate to be in your boots when Cole Stockton hears that ya'll robbed kinfolk to his woman friend. Why, Cole Stockton would be on yore trail faster than flies on stink. He would hunt you down, lock you up, and throw away the keys—that is, iffen he don't shoot you down like the crazy dog fools that you are first."

Both Zeb and Tom Wooley suddenly felt sickly in their stomachs They turned to glare with bloodshot eyes at their brother, Mort. Once again, Mort had used his persuasion to start a situation that he couldn't finish, and had brought his older brothers into it.

Zeb yelled, "Mort, you idiot! We ought to smack the living daylights out've you. You would have us rob kinfolk to Marshal Stockton's woman? Kinfolk to the United States Marshal's woman? Have you got holes in your head? You must, cause your brains sure must have leaked out."

Mort sat wide-eyed and unbelieving. He only knew these people had money. If only he had taken a few minutes longer at the Denver station, he would have overheard the rest of the conversation. He would have learned who they were and that their destination was the Sumner Ranch.

Mort was dumbfounded and mute, so Zeb thought hard for a long moment. "All right, driver, we made a mistake. There'll be no robbery today. Get your coach out've our sight." The brothers turned their horses away from the coach and reined in.

The wise old driver clucked to his team, and once again, the coach lurched forward on its way to the Lower Colorado. The guard turned to see Sammy Colter grinning as the coach moved out of hearing range. He asked, "Sammy, why did you tell them that?"

Sammy smiled as he replied, "Them boys don't usually mean any harm. They's just down on their luck, as well as just plain stupid. Besides, I shore didn't want them looking in the boot. As you know, Agent Danson put that strong box on board before we left Denver. We are carrying close to ten thousand dollars in gold."

Sammy glanced back over his shoulder just then to watch the two brothers jerk Mort off his mount and commence thrashing him good. Sammy couldn't help laughing out loud.

"Come on now team, Hee-Hawh!"

The team moved into a fast trot, and both driver and guard laughed about the encounter for the next several miles. The passengers were awestruck by the manner in which the crusty old stagecoach driver had saved them from robbery. Their estimation of the driver tripled. He had experience in this God-forsaken landscape that quite possibly saved their lives, not to mention their valuables.

CHAPTER THREE

Cole and Bodine

I rose with the first rays of the sun that morning. After dressing and gathering up my trail gear, a quick cup of coffee sent me down to the barn to greet my chestnut stallion. I saddled Warrior and secured my gear on the saddle. I slipped my Winchester into the scabbard and led Warrior out of the barn.

Laura's foreman, Judd Ellison, approached from the bunkhouse. He called out, "Morning, Cole! Going for an early ride?"

"Good morning to you also, Judd. Yes. Actually, it's a journey. I received a message from Judge Wilkerson at the territorial court. Says that he has something really important to talk with me about. He asked that I bring Toby Bodine with me. We should be back in about a week's time."

I mounted Warrior with a quick wave of adios to Judd who waved back his acknowledgement. Touching spur lightly to Warrior's flank, he broke into a frisky trot. He seemed anxious to travel. I believe he sensed that this trip would be a long ride.

I caught up with Toby at the jailhouse. Prior to traveling, we stopped in at Lucy Todd's café for a bite of breakfast. While waiting for our order, over coffee, Toby broke the silence with, "Cole, do you know what the judge wants with us?"

I responded with, "No, Toby, I don't. But, it must be important. He never sends me a telegram unless he needs something quickly. Well, no matter, we'll find out when we get there. By the way, Toby, I think that we should stop by the town of Creedence on our return. There is someone I know there that I believe you should meet."

Bodine had a questioning look on his face. My reply was only a grin. The waitress appeared momentarily with our meal and the coffee pot.

To tell the truth, I had been thinking often lately of Allyson. She was a pretty young lady that I met during my first trip to Creedence.

Toby was near to her age, and although I'd not played cupid before, I thought that they might become fast friends.

It was late afternoon three days hence when we rode up and dismounted at the Territorial Courthouse in Denver. We tied Warrior and Toby's mount at the hitching rack, and then entered the stone building. Not delaying to clean up before going to the courthouse, we tramped up the steps and approached Judge Wilkerson's outer office.

"Good afternoon, Henry. We are here at the judge's request. Might he see us now?"

Henry, the court clerk, looked up over his wire-rimmed spectacles and grinned. "Hello, Marshal Stockton, Deputy Bodine. Yes, His Honor is quite anxious to see the both of you. Wait here a moment."

Henry stood, then walked to the door of the private chamber. He was gone only a minute or so before he returned and ushered us directly in to see Judge Wilkerson. Henry stayed in the office with us, obviously expecting directions or expecting to share in the moment.

The old purveyor of justice rose and stepped around his desk and held his hand out to us. After a warm handshake, he spoke. "Cole! Toby! Come and sit down. We'll have a sip of my private stock—in celebration."

Toby and I exchanged glances. "What exactly are we celebrating?" we both asked almost in unison.

A wide smile came over Wilkerson's face and he nodded his head. "Cole, I have papers in my hand appointing you as THE United States Marshal for the Colorado Territory. Bodine is now relieved of his assignment up north. I am assigning him to be your Chief Deputy Marshal. You two will now be the federal law around these parts. Well, Toby, do you think that you would like to work with Cole?"

"I can't think of anyone better to learn from," replied Toby.

The old hand of justice chuckled, "Hand over that deputy star, Cole. From now on, you will wear this one."

I handed the Judge my Deputy U.S. Marshal star. After placing it on his desk, he stepped forward and with deft movement, pinned the silver star of United States Marshal on my shirtfront. Then he pumped my hand and congratulated me. Toby followed suit, and then Henry was there with his firm hand for me and my new deputy.

Refusing Henry's offer to serve, the judge then moved to his sideboard and withdrew four glasses and a decanter. When each of us had a glass in hand, His Honor looked directly at Toby and me, raised his glass and offered, "Fellows, I have every confidence that you two will do the Territory of Colorado proud. The people of this territory are fortunate to have you two working together for law, order, and justice."

And then, we hoisted glasses to taste a very smooth prime whiskey. After a few more pleasantries, it was time to return to our duties.

* *

Following our visit with Wilkerson, Toby and I made our way out of the courthouse and mounted up. My mind was still somewhat a blur of events. I was no longer a Deputy U.S. Marshal. I was now The United States Marshal for the Territory of Colorado. It would take some getting used to.

Bodine eyed me and with a mischievous grin blurted out, "Where to now, Boss Marshal?" I turned Warrior up the street and trotted on out. Toby was right beside me as we made our way south out of the city. From Denver, we rode south towards Pueblo. Toby was in the dark, but he asked no questions.

The farming community of Creedence lay some fifteen miles east of Pueblo in the area of the Colorado Great Plains. The majestic Rocky Mountains lay to the west of Pueblo. This land to the east was some of the most fertile in the country.

It had been some time since I had made a call on the Millers. I knew that Lucy Miller loved to cook for visitors. Lucy was one of those Western women who could take a piece of the toughest meat and turn it into a mouth-watering meal. I envisioned that Allyson would give me one of those hugs that made the long trip worthwhile and Vern Miller would open up one of his jugs that he kept on hand for special occasions.

The following afternoon, we dismounted at the post on the lawn in front of the Miller home. Before we could step up on the porch, a flash of flowered print dress and flying auburn hair rushed out the door, jumped right up into my arms, and planted a big one on my cheek.

Toby stood there wide-eyed and dumbfounded. I could tell by the slack of his jaw that he was interested. Vern and Lucy Miller stepped out onto the porch, and introduced themselves to Toby. They each sized up this young man in my company. Who was he?

I said, "Toby, this here's Allyson. Isn't she a mighty pretty girl? She can cook up a storm, too, just like her mother."

Toby removed his hat, and with a sweeping bow that caused Vern and Lucy to grin from ear to ear, related his immense pleasure at meeting this charming young woman. I saw the looks that passed between them and I couldn't help but chuckle.

Lucy Miller made the next move, "Come on in and make yourselves to home."

She didn't have to say that twice. I could smell the baked goods and unmistakable aroma of freshly brewed coffee. Up the porch we went and into the house, spurs jingling.

First off, I eyed a platter of fresh baked donuts, cinnamon rolls, and a pie on the sideboard. Well, I'd tasted of Lucy's apple pie before, and there was none better, that is, unless it was a thick slice of Laura's homemade berry pie. A few minutes later, we had a couple of donuts and some mighty good coffee. I took note that Allyson made it a point to sit next to Toby and every so often would steal an appraising glance at him.

"You must stay for supper," announced Vern, "and afterwards, we'll find a place around the fireplace. We'll have a taste of some special vintage and talk of the news around the Territory."

After supper, we men folk gathered around the fireplace, and spoke of the news. Toby couldn't wait to tell about my new appointment. Lucy and Allyson picked up and washed the dishes while listening to the conversation. Lucy added a comment or question now and then.

I glanced casually over my shoulder to find Allyson's eyes following Toby's every move. I could see the excitement in her eyes, and now I knew what Taylor Thornton was speaking of when he observed Laura and me together.

An idea hit my mind just then, and I turned to Toby. "Why don't you stay around Creedence for a week or so. You can get the lay of the land. Introduce yourself to Sheriff Brad Maxwell. Maxwell will be glad to meet you, and he could find a room for you at Daisy Martin's Boarding House. I'm sure that the Miller family will introduce you to the people around here. Let them know who and what you are. I'll ride back to Laura's place, and we'll see you in a few days."

I looked at Vern and he was slightly nodding his head as he smoked his corncob pipe. He winked at Lucy, and she had a bright glimmer in her eyes. It was like she had known from the start that this young man, Toby, was right for her Allyson.

Well, the smiles that spread across both Toby's and Allyson's faces were well worth the lonesome trip back. That they would become very close friends was evident.

When it was time for sleep, Toby and I stabled our animals and brought in our saddle rolls. We spread them out before the fireplace and made ourselves comfortable. At daylight, we were up with the family as they began readying for the day's farm chores.

Lucy Miller made up a great trail breakfast of hotcakes, bacon and eggs. There was lots of good hot black coffee. I felt fit as a fiddle when I put boot to stirrup and swung into the saddle. Toby and the Miller family waved farewell as I turned back toward the road to Laura's ranch.

Warrior and I traveled at an easy pace toward Miller's Station and Laura's place. I was grateful for this rare opportunity to enjoy the scenery and good weather. My mind returned more than once to the Miller farm. Toby and Allyson were becoming acquainted. What interests did they share? Both of them held strong family values. Would it evolve into a strong relationship like Laura's and mine? Then, I thought of Laura. It would be good to be at home.

Warrior and I had traveled some twenty miles when I caught the glimpse of three riders camped off the road up in the tree line. They looked to have coffee on, and I caught scent of a noonday meal frying up. I figured that they might have spare a cup of coffee, so I swung up the incline and hailed the camp.

W-e-l-l, those guys turned out to be the Wooley brothers and boy were they fidgety. I rode right up to their camp. All three of their faces were white as a sheet. When I dismounted to face them, they all stood and raised their hands.

"Don't shoot, Marshal Stockton. We give up. We didn't know that that there woman on the Overland coach was kin to Miss Sumner—honest. We really didn't mean no harm to no one. We's just out of work and mighty hungry."

I looked each of them in the eyes and inquired, "What are you fellows talking about?"

All talking at once, they made an effort to fill me in. I had to turn my head to keep from laughing. I'd known this family for a few years and if there was hard luck around, it was sure to find the Wooleys.

I sighed deeply. These boys were down on their luck, but still needed a lesson. A few days in jail would keep them out of mischief, and besides, the Territory could spare a few meals.

"OK, boys. You done wrong, but I ain't got time to take you in. I want you to break camp and ride over to Creedence. Tell my deputy, Toby Bodine, that I said to lock you boys up for five days. At the end of those five days, I want you to ride over to the Widow Hooper's place. You tell her that I sent you to help out with anything that needs done."

"Yes sir, Marshal Stockton. We'll be there," they chorused. I knew they would.

We all recalled that Mrs. Hooper lost her husband to a bad heart a year or so back and badly needed help to keep her farm up and running. Besides—word had it that she fixed the best rabbit stew this side of St. Louis. Those boys would sure do their best to keep on the good side of that cooking.

Once again, I swung into the saddle, another grin spreading across my face. Anticipation of Laura's embrace was good reason to ride.

CHAPTER FOUR

Dandies Arrive at Miller's Station

Laura Sumner spent the next several days overseeing preparation for her cousin's visit. The ranch house, bunkhouse, stables and barn received fresh coats of pain. Corrals and fences were repaired.

The *Boss Lady* directed that the ranch wagon be painted, as well as all harnesses repaired. Extra saddles were soaped, and made ready. Flowerbeds were weeded, and another couple of chairs were built, painted, and added to the porch furniture. The bar-b-que pit was cleaned up, and re-lined with large stones.

Laura baked several batches of cookies and rolls. The aroma of fresh baked goods filled the ranch yard. Her boys would stopped work every so often to sniff the air. The aroma was invigorating.

"Hope she saves some of those cookies for us," mused one of her wranglers.

At dusk, Laura had the boys sit with her on the porch with coffee while she schooled them somewhat in the art of *gentlemanly* manners. Much to the wrangler's delight, the lessons were served with a passel of cookies and coffee.

She also reminded them that during the next two weeks, they each had to wash up daily. These were wranglers—accustomed to cleaning up only on special occasions, like Saturday night flings—whether they felt that they needed it or not.

She asked them to shave every morning during her cousin's visit, and to trim hair and mustaches neatly. Above all, they must have clean clothes every morning while her cousin was there. The boys scowled a bit; however, they agreed to everything, well, almost everything.

Now, everyone knows that when dudes come west, they are sure targets for *funning*, and other such pranks of crafty and devious nature. Laura reluctantly agreed to let the boys drum up some kind of *initiation* fun for the visitors—providing that no one got hurt.

The boys agreed, and Laura searched all of their faces, glancing from one to another. A twinkle in their eyes made her a little uneasy. The wranglers returned her smile with devilish grins that announced a week of good ole horse wrangling fun and games.

* *

The Stinson's special coach finally arrived in the small town an hour's ride from Laura's ranch. Sammy Colter halted the coach directly in front of the hotel and announced, "Miller's Station! You can get room and board inside."

The dusty, rumpled, sweat streaked trio stepped with less than steady gait out of the coach, and looked around. They scowled as they surveyed the bare board false front buildings that lined the single dusty street.

"How could anyone live in a place like this?" exclaimed Victoria.

Walter, without a word, viewed the range of merchants along the street front, and mentally counted the saloons—five of them to be exact. There were five saloons, one fairly large hotel, a jailhouse, a livery stable, a general mercantile store, one blacksmith shop, two restaurants, one small café, one feed-seed-and-grain store, and a combination stagecoach, telegraph office, and express station. That was it. That was the town.

Here they were, the three of them dressed in quality attire, and this was the town. Local folks standing near the mercantile always gaped at strangers off the stage. The three strangers brought hushed small talk from the locals. Who were they? Why were they at Miller's Station? A few young children ran down the street to get a better look at these newcomers.

"You there! Yes, you," addressed Mason to one of the local townspeople, "We are here to visit with Miss Laura Sumner—she has a ranch near here. How do we get there?"

"W-e-l-l," replied the old gentleman as he stroked his grey whiskers, "I guess we could send a rider out there to let them know you are here. Take a body about an hour's good riding there and another hour back. Ya'll might get a room at the hotel across the street. Either of the restaurants has good home cooking. I'm sure that Miss Sumner will send someone to fetch ya'll in the morning."

"YES, Walter!" stated Victoria, "I WANT A BATH and some clean clothes; and some decent food. I feel like I am carrying a pound of that trail dirt on me, and my clothes are wringing wet. I smell like that musty old stagecoach, and I AM HUNGRY. WE WILL GET A ROOM and ready ourselves to visit tomorrow."

Walter agreed. Besides, he wanted a good stiff drink to wash down all that trail dust that he was sure that he swallowed. He wanted a bath and a shave as well. Walter felt repulsed that he must smell like the horses that pulled the coach.

Mason, on the other hand, was the product of a farm family in New Jersey. He was beginning to feel as though he was a young man again at the sight of this town. He had traveled to New York City as a young man. At the insistence of his father, he had attended an academy for gentlemen.

Mason evolved from a farm lad into a gentleman's man, and languished in his elegance. Now, at the sight of this small Lower Colorado town, he felt the tug of his roots. He imagined himself living here, but he dare not mention it to Victoria or Walter.

The Stinson entourage registered at the hotel. Victoria was surprised that the rooms were most accommodating. The rooms were clean and well furnished. The beds seemed comfortable enough. However, they were required to bathe in a washroom down the hall.

Victoria naturally got the tub first, and she breathed a sigh of delight as she slowly slipped into the heated water with scented bath soap. She closed her eyes, and dreamed for an instant of her luxurious claw footed tub at home. Oh, if only she were home in her own bath, immersed in salts from Paris, rather than this galvanized tub. This modest adaptation would do for now.

Walter requested the hotel clerk send for a bottle of whiskey. He and Mason sat in the butler's room sipping the amber liquid from glasses found in the room. It was strong, and burned on the way down—but tasted good to both men.

Eighteen year old, Billy Gaines, the livery stable helper had offered to ride out to Laura's ranch and announce their arrival. Billy had been quick to volunteer for the task since Laura always had some of the best milk and cookies on hand. His mouth watered at the thought as he saddled up the livery's young gray mare. He mounted, and led out toward the ranch at an easy trot.

* *

An hour later, Billy rode easy into Laura's ranch yard and dismounted in front of the freshly painted white porch. He smelled the aroma of freshly baked cookies. Would Laura allow him a couple for his effort? He tramped up the steps and rapped lightly on the door.

Laura Sumner appeared and greeted the young man. "Hi, Billy, what brings you here?"

"Well, Miss Sumner, there's some mighty strange looking folks in town—came in this afternoon on a special coach from Denver. They are dressed mighty fancy like—a bit dusty mind you—but fancy like."

Billy smiled as he continued, "There's two men and a real pretty lady. They said that their name was Stinson. The lady said that she was kin to you. Anyways, they will be staying at the hotel tonight. They would like to find a means to come out to your ranch tomorrow. Miss Laura, those cookies smell real good. Do you think you could spare a couple—and a glass of milk?"

"Come on, Billy, you've earned them. Take a half dozen. Ride back to town and tell those folks that someone will come into town and meet them at around nine o'clock tomorrow morning. There will be a wagon for them to ride in out to the ranch."

"Oh, by the way, Miss Laura," stammered Billy, "their luggage will take up an entire wagon by itself."

"Oh, Lord," uttered Laura under her breath.

Billy eagerly scooped up a handful of Laura's freshly baked cookies and sauntered out the door, munching away and mumbling the details that the ranch lady had given him. Laura watched him ride out, and then walked over to the bunkhouse to lay out the arrival plans to her wranglers. Once again she would call on them for assistance.

CHAPTER FIVE

Cousins Meet

Early morning found Judd Ellison standing in front of the ranch house dressed in a starched shirt, Levi's, and string tie. His boots were polished, and he looked quite the *gentleman*. Judd had the ranch wagon hitched and waiting for Laura to appear.

Two other riders, namely Mike Wilkes and Juan Soccoro, stood to horse. They were likewise cleaned up and attired in fresh shirts and Levi's. They would ride along just in case they were needed. Soon, the front door of the ranch house opened and a vision of loveliness emerged.

Laura wore an attractive long flowing navy skirt, white blouse buttoned to the collar, with waist jacket. An ivory broach pinned to a navy velvet ribbon around her neck complimented the outfit. Her hair cascaded softly over her shoulders and down her back. She was breathtakingly beautiful and the boys each let out with a resounding "Whew!"

Laura blushed slightly at the display, but took a deep breath and responded in a cheerful voice, "OK, boys, let's go get my cousin."

Judd helped Laura into the wagon, and then climbed up beside her to drive. Mike and Juan swung into the saddle, and followed them out the gate at an easy lope.

An hour later, Laura and her wranglers rolled into town. The special Overland coach was already hitched up and waiting in front of the hotel. Sammy Colter stood by his team cutting himself a new chaw. His face lit up with a big smile when he saw Laura.

"Good morning, Miss Laura," he drawled, "I reckon I brought you some visitors yesterday."

"Good morning, Sammy. Yes. Did they have a pleasant trip?"

Sammy chuckled a bit and answered, "Sort of. It was kind of touch and go there for a while. But, they's all in one piece—least they were last night. My, my, but you sure do look a sight for these tired old eyes."

Laura blushed, smiled, and dropped her glance to the ground for an instant.

Sammy continued, "Miss Laura. I knowed your old Uncle Jesse. Good man. He knew what he was doing when he willed that ranch to you. Them folks inside don't know nothing about the West. Anyway, I guess I'll be driving them out to your ranch. Ya'll got room in the bunk house for one more, I hope."

Jud Ellison chuckled. "Yes, Sammy. There's always room for one more at the Sumner Ranch."

After the small talk, Laura and Judd left Sammy at the coach to make their way to the hotel lobby. Two finely dressed gents and a woman about Laura's age sat at the far end of the lobby near the fireplace. The trio rose as Laura approached. The two men eyed Laura appreciatively. The woman's eyes reflected admiration, although with a slight hint of envy.

"She's beautiful," thought Laura.

"She's beautiful," thought Victoria before breaking the momentary trance. "Hello. You must be Laura. I am your cousin Victoria. This is my husband Walter. And, this is our gentleman Mason. We have been most anxious to meet you and to spend some time with you on YOUR ranch."

Laura couldn't help but notice the inflection in Victoria's voice. She quickly turned to introduce Judd to the group. After formalities, the party went out to the coach and wagon.

Laura motioned to Mike Wilkes and Juan Soccorro to retrieve the pile of luggage that sat stacked on the boardwalk. The boys made their way to the luggage and began to place everything in the back of the ranch wagon. Juan looked at Mike and sighed.

"Mi Amigo, I have never in my life seen so much baggage for three people. Did they bring everything they own?"

"I donno, Juan. But it seems to me that they intend on staying longer than a week or so. More like a year or so—maybe two."

Mason and Judd assisted the ladies into the coach door. Laura sat inside the coach with Victoria, Walter, and Mason while Judd climbed up on the high box with Sammy Colter. Juan and Mike rode in the heavily laden ranch wagon, their horses trailing at the rear.

With all aboard and baggage accounted for, the entourage rumbled out of town toward the Sumner Horse Ranch.

Victoria chattered incessantly about their trip and about how dastardly the accommodations were all along the journey.

"Laura, I can't begin to tell you about how unpleasant this journey was for us. The rail travel was long and tedious. It seemed that the further west we traveled, the more unsavory characters boarded our train. Thank goodness, we traveled in an elite first class passenger car." Laura could only nod before Victoria continued about the stagecoach ride.

"And, I absolutely abhorred the musty stagecoach ride from Denver to your fair town. Would you believe that we traveled through swarms of pesky insects, not to mention that that driver made us get out and walk alongside the coach at times? To rest the horses he said."

Victoria's eyes rolled up a moment as she collected her thoughts, "Stagecoach station food is deplorable. Just imagine! They tried to serve us wild animal meat for supper. I took one taste and almost got sick. Well, they did make amends and provided me some warmed over chicken, or that is what I think it was."

Laura thought back to her own stagecoach travel and thought, "The antelope steak that I had was delicious. In fact, the venison breakfast steak with eggs was delightful. Victoria just doesn't know what a great experience she could have had, had she given the meals a chance."

Finally, Victoria spoke about accommodations at the stagecoach overnight stations. "The air in this territory is clear and cold. But, those itchy wool blankets drove me almost insane. I never got a good night's sleep the entire trip. I certainly hope that you have some decent blankets for our visit."

Basically, Laura spoke when given the chance to get a word in edgewise, and assured Victoria that the ranch was a beautiful place to be. She spoke of the panoramic view of the snow-capped mountains, the fresh fragrance of pine trees and wild flowers, nature's creatures, and of course—the fresh air.

Laura beamed when she mentioned, like most women do, of her special friend—Cole Stockton. Victoria was all ears. She wanted to meet this man called Stockton.

Almost as an afterthought, "Oh, yes," remarked Victoria, "I met a couple of ladies in town at the hotel yesterday evening, and I invited them to have tea with us this afternoon at your ranch. I do hope that you don't mind."

"Yes, Victoria. That would be fine. Who did you invite?"

"Let's see now. Leah Torney, Agnes Gearheart, Anne Tatum, and Sarah Bishop. They all told me that they know you."

Laura knew them all right. They were the most dedicated busy bodies of the entire community, and cousin Victoria had just invited them all into her ranch—to be more exact—her home.

"Damn!" thought Laura. "What luck!"

At last, the coach pulled into the gates of the Sumner Ranch and came to a halt in front of the house. Judd Ellison climbed down from the box and opened the door of the old coach.

The gentlemen climbed out first and then Judd helped Victoria and Laura to the ground. Juan and Mike called for other hands to help unload the luggage from the wagon.

Victoria stepped away from the coach, stopped in her tracks and gazed slowly around at the ranch. She took in its freshly painted porch, the flowerbeds, and the corrals with several horses lazing about. She peered intently at the Rocky Mountain skyline. A sense of peace enveloped her. She had never known a place like this.

Mason assisted the wranglers with the luggage, holding his own out. Afterward, he accompanied Mike Wilkes and Juan Soccoro to the bunkhouse. The Eastern couple's gentleman looked forward to his adventure with the wranglers.

Victoria and Walter followed Laura inside the house where she showed them to the spare room. It was quaint, with flowery curtains at the windows. Laura also showed them the washroom where the simple galvanized tub stood. Victoria shuddered at the thought of another two weeks without her personal tub.

"Oh, well," she thought, "I will have to make do. It won't be forever." She turned to smile at Laura. "Come, Laura, dear. Let's prepare for our welcoming tea. I suppose that you have a gentleman to take care of everything for you—if not, we can put Mason in charge. He is a master at setting out tea."

"That sounds fine," replied Laura, and in the back of her mind was "a gentleman to fix tea and cookies? I'll bet that she's never gotten her dainty lily white hands dirty over a camp fire, or a cook stove. She wouldn't have the slightest notion what to do with supper dishes, or washing clothes, or pitching hay, or feeding stock, or—or—there must be a hundred things she cannot do. I wonder if she really knows how to ride a horse." Laura's mind raced with thoughts of this inept person.

Around two o'clock in the afternoon two buggies with the four townswomen rolled through the gates of Laura's ranch. The women were dressed in their finest attire, as though they were the epitome of Miller's Station's society. As Victoria had earlier, they too took in the surroundings.

"So, this is old Jesse's place," mused Anne Tatum.

Sarah Bishop was quick responding with, "Miss Laura surely gave the old place a new look."

None of the women had ever been to the Sumner Ranch before. They were amazed at how peaceful it appeared. They knew Laura as a horsewoman, but had somehow never figured her for the makings of a lady of good breeding. The ranch proved them wrong. It held the aura of beauty. From their vantage point in the buggies, the house had the grace of a woman's touch.

They climbed down from their buggies, then walked up the steps to the porch. Everything had its place. The porch furniture was so quaint. Each could imagine sitting out on this porch at dusk, watching the sun go down in the west while sipping a cup of hot coffee or tea. How lovely the mountains were without the buildings of town and neighbors close by to ruin the view!

Victoria met them at the door. She wore an afternoon frock, perfect for an at-home tea. Each guest stared with envy at the soft colors and modern style.

"Come in, come in," sang Victoria. "Tea is just about ready, and we have some of the most delicious cookies I have ever tasted."

The ladies of the Lower Colorado, who thought themselves superior socially, took notice of Laura's ranch house the moment they stepped inside. Slowly, each surveyed the large living room. They were overwhelmed that a horsewoman such as Laura would keep a home so nicely.

Her furnishings were tasteful and welcoming. Each lady felt comfortable and happy to be invited, even though it was at the invitation of a stranger. This Laura Sumner was quite a woman.

The curtains were a subdued floral. Freshly cut wild flowers cascaded from a vase on a dining table. Photographs of Laura's family in Texas graced the mantle alongside a photo of Jesse Sumner. A comfortable horsehair sofa was positioned in front of the large fireplace.

There were, of course, the typical tools of late nineteenth century ranch life near the door. A Henry repeating rifle hung over the door, and a double barreled shotgun rested in a corner next to the front window.

A coat tree stood next to the door and on it hung a gun belt. The loops of the belt were filled with .38 caliber cartridges, and the Colt Lightning Revolver sitting in the holster was well cared for. They had each seen this gun belt before—settled around Laura's small waist.

Laura greeted them each with a smile and her usual grace. Victoria led the conversation. She introduced Walter who quickly excused himself. He was accustomed to being the center of attention at men's gatherings, but there were no men at this function. After the trip out from Miller's Station and Victoria's constant chatter, he was ready for a nap.

Mason puttered around the kitchen putting the finishing touches on the platter of cookies, aligning the teacups, and making sure that all was a matter of the utmost Eastern etiquette.

At last, Mason served the tea and cookies. The ladies spoke of having a welcoming social dance in one of their homes. It would be in recognition of their new friends, Victoria and Walter.

The social was scheduled for the following Saturday. Everyone who was anyone in the Lower Colorado Society would be invited. Victoria felt like a queen reigning over her subjects. Little did she know that the new acquaintances were ordinary townspeople— wives of farmers and ranchers, who positioned themselves as society, not that they were. Most of them had been raised in the wilds of the Colorado.

Laura thought, "Oh, Lord, Victoria hasn't been here but a few hours and already she is overseeing what she deems formal social functions. I wonder how Cole will react to attending a social with my kin from the East?"

CHAPTER SIX

Cole Returns to the LS Ranch

I had been traveling steady since morning and was ready for a bath, a shave, and a cup of Laura's good hot coffee when I rode through the gate to her ranch. Much to my surprise, there were two buggies hitched at the post in front of the house. I couldn't help thinking something was wrong. Why all the visitors? Judd Ellison waited on the bottom step.

It appeared that something mighty peculiar was going on here. Judd wore a jacket and tie. His boots were polished. I thought, "What in tarnation is was going on here? A funeral? A wedding?"

I pulled up to the hitching post and before I could dismount, Judd quickly stepped over to me.

"What is going on here?" I questioned anxiously.

"Laura and her cousin from New York City are having afternoon tea, Cole."

"A tea party?" I asked incredulously.

"Yes, Cole, a tea party. Laura's cousin Victoria from back East in New York City arrived here last night with her husband, a gentleman's man, would you believe, and about a ton of luggage. Laura had me move your things over to the bunkhouse with the wranglers and me. You are bunking next to me."

Judd took a moment to let that sink in; then, he continued, "This here gentleman's man is staying with us and so is Sammy Colter, the Overland stagecoach driver. Walter hired the coach in Denver. Laura arranged for the local agent to loan it to us for the week or so that they will be here. She asked me to watch for you, and requested that you clean up before coming to the house. Cole, please knock before entering and wait for Laura's response. I reminded her that you were always a gentleman."

"Well, Judd, with these instructions, I understand. Laura must be ashamed that we are together. I'll respect her wishes though and get cleaned up. If she sticks her head out of the door, let her know that I am back, and will be to the house as quickly as I can."

I was more than a little miffed that Laura would even think of putting on airs. This was not the Laura that I knew. Victoria must be something else to cause Laura to panic. Surely, she was not herself. Anyways, I trotted on over to the barn, saw to Warrior with an extra bait of oats, and then shuffled over to the bunkhouse.

Sammy Colter was resting on a lower bunk with a fresh chaw of tobacco.

"Howdy, Marshal Stockton," he called out. "Guess you know about the company by now. I take it that is your bunk over by the window. The boys wouldn't let nobody near it. Told that there fancy feller, Mason, to keep his things offen it, it being taken and all."

"Thanks, Sammy. How long you been here?"

"Since yesterday. Almost got held up by them Wooley brothers, but I outfoxed them. They don't mean no harm, Marshal, you know that."

"Yah, Sammy. I met them on the trail. They sort of filled me in on their escapades. I sent them up to Creedence to spend a few days in jail and then to do some chores for Mrs. Hooper. You know she needs help on that place."

Sammy chuckled a mite, and then showed further amusement as he thought more about the Wooley boys. His guffawed belly laughs brought tears of laughter to his eyes.

I laid out my suit, a fresh shirt, and string tie. I figured that I might as well dress like everyone else—to make an impression, just this once, for Laura. Besides, I wanted to see firsthand just what in the devil was going on.

* *

About an hour later, I stepped up on the porch and rapped lightly on the door. A fancy dressed gentleman opened the door and inquired who I was, and what my business was with the occupants.

Now, that got my curiosity up. I announced myself as "Cole Stockton, a friend of Miss Laura Sumner."

In the back of my mind, I wanted to say, "I am Cole Stockton, and I live here. Just who the hell are you?"

The next thing out of the stranger's mouth was, "Sir, you are wearing a side arm. Will you remove it before entering?"

"Not likely," I answered, and pushed by him to make my way to the living room. All eyes were on me.

"Howdy folks," I said, "Sure could use a cup of hot coffee."

Laura rose and walked over to me. She read my eyes, hesitated only a moment, and then introduced me to everyone. The ladies of the town knew me, of course, thus acknowledged with a smile and a nod.

Walter returned to the living room. He extended his hand. I shook it firmly. He seemed glad to have another man in the room. Victoria was indeed an attractive woman. She had an air about her that warned me to walk carefully in her sight.

Victoria sized me up and down. A wry smile slowly spread across her face. She would be a trial for any man.

Following introductions, Laura slipped into the kitchen to get that coffee for me. I was left on my own amongst the Eastern and Lower Colorado social butterflies. Walter appeared to be a patsy pushover who took his marching orders from his wife.

Victoria was quite forward in her conversation with me. She hinted that I should take her riding some morning within the week. She gushed about seeing the magnificent beauty of a glorious Western morning. W-e-l-l, that would set the tongues of the Lower Colorado Territory socialites a-wagging.

Walter pretty near choked on his cookies at the inference, and sipped on the steaming hot tea in order to wash down the goodies. That caused him to quickly inhale to cool his throat, and Mason rushed to him with a glass of cool water to ease the awkward situation.

Mason glanced at me with this smirk on his face as if he knew something that I didn't. It was one of those "You'll find out soon enough" looks.

Laura returned to the living room about that time with my coffee. I was surprised that it was in a cup and saucer. I took a sip before clearing my throat. I apprised her of Victoria's request.

I could see it in Laura's eyes—if looks could kill, then Victoria would be dead. However, Laura kept the composure of a gracious hostess. She responded with, "YES, Cole. If anyone should show Victoria the countryside, it should be a man who rides the wild trails every day. One who could protect her appropriately should some danger find her. Yes, Cole, I think that you should take Victoria riding. She may ride Brandy."

Well, there it was. Victoria had succeeded. Laura was more that a bit jealous.

"What the hell," I thought. "There couldn't be that much harm in a short friendly ride around the ranch, could there?"

Some two hours after arriving, the ladies from the Lower Colorado departed with enough gossip to keep them busy for several days to come.

Laura waited until the ladies had left, then announced that supper would be special tonight, for Juan Soccorro and his wife Emilita would prepare the evening meal. They were eager to prepare Southwestern dishes to tease the taste buds.

Victoria readily admitted, "I don't believe that either Walter or I have ever partaken of a Southwestern style meal." Mason acknowledged that he had not either.

Laura commented, "Southwestern fare is a bit spicy. Should you not care for the cuisine, Emilita will provide something more to your taste. She is an excellent cook."

Each of the guests expressed their desire to sample Emilita's south of the border fare. Laura looked to the clock over the mantle, and suggested, "Supper should be served in about an hour. Perhaps you would like to stroll around the ranch yard. I'd like to show you a few points of interest."

Victoria agreed, "Lead the way, dear Laura. We would love to have a guided tour of this beautiful ranch."

The group rose and followed Laura out the door to the porch. I held back and brought up the rear. She led them around to the left side of the house and pointed out the grassy knoll where a few markers stood. Of particular note was the area with a white picket fence that stood apart from the rest of the graves. Laura related, "Jesse is buried inside the white fence." She looked at Victoria, "Anytime you want to go up there, I will go with you, if you would like me to."

Victoria was silent, but Laura could see the slight tremble of her lower lip and the emotional struggle in her eyes. Victoria slowly shook her head, then brightened up and bid Laura to continue the tour.

Laura nodded and led out toward the barn and stables. The aroma of Emilita's cooking floated lightly on the air and I inhaled of it deeply. I noticed that others did likewise.

As we walked, Laura pointed out the scenery to all four points of the compass. "And, in the distance, at the foot of the Rocky Mountains is where we find most of our horses to wrangle and train to saddle."

Once at the stables and corrals, Laura proudly showed off her favorite black horse. "This is Mickey, he is my most favorite mount. I have another, however; Sultan is the leader of a small herd out on the range. He brings them in near here every so often."

Victoria peered over the next stall to be met by a chestnut blazed face. "And, who does this animal belong to?" Grinning, I answered, "Warrior is my horse."

I could see that she was attracted to Warrior. "Go ahead," I invited, "stroke his face."

Warrior seemed to like her touch. He moved forward and lowered his sleek neck a bit to give her full access to his entire head. I glanced over to Laura. She slightly nodded approval of Victoria's interest.

Next, we moved to the end of the corrals. In the large ocean of grass grazed some thirty animals of various color and size. The Easterners were duly impressed as Laura explained how her boys caught, wrangled the wild out of them, and tamed them to saddle mounts.

"This bunch was recently tamed. However, in the other pasture to the left of the stables, there are ten horses to be worked. Tomorrow, you will see the wranglers do their work. I believe that you will show as much enthusiasm as we do."

A kitchen triangle sounded. Juan called out that supper was almost ready to serve. Laura led us back to the house where everyone could quickly wash up before the meal.

* *

We gathered in the dining room to find a fine linen tablecloth spread with a vase of wild flowers as the centerpiece. A light fragrance filled room. The table was set with Laura's simple dinner plates and tableware. Even so, it represented our Lower Colorado life style.

We took our places. I sat at one end of the table with Laura seated opposite me. Presently, Juan Soccorro appeared attired as a caballero. He struck a dashing figure, dressed in colorful red and black Mexican short jacket with white shirt and bolo tie. He held a carafe of homemade wild berry wine that Laura's colored wrangler, Jeff Sutton, broke out from his private supply. Juan poured the wine into our glasses with ease.

Next, Emilita appeared in a flowered skirt and white blouse. She held a large platter of meat. As she placed the platter in front of me, she spoke in pleasant voice, "My friends, my people call *carne asada*. From an old recipe of my mother. I hope you enjoy."

Juan joined her with bowls of Mexican rice and savory vegetables from Laura's garden. He commented as he placed the large bowl of rice near the center of the table, "This is called in Mexico, *arroz roja* or red rice.

To state it in simple terms, everyone enjoyed the meal. I could not recall the last time that I feasted on Emilita's south of the border fare. Afterward, Juan served coffee while Emilita brought generous servings of Laura's fine wild berry cobbler.

I learned later that Laura had ensured a second berry cobbler went to the bunkhouse so that her boys wouldn't be left out. Yes, that was Laura. I'd said it many times before. Laura's wranglers were the best fed in the Territory.

After supper, we men moved to the front porch where Walter and Mason lit up cigars. I rolled out a smoke and lit up. Laura and Victoria moved to the living room while Juan and Emilita cleaned up the dining room and kitchen.

It was near midnight when Laura's guests retired for the night. Laura and I finally got to sit together with coffee on the porch. We needed to talk. She apprised me of the entire situation as she saw it.

"Cole, I know you feel uncomfortable. But, I feel that I need to show Victoria that I am truly a lady. She needs to know that I am her equal in social graces."

"Laura," I replied, "you don't need to show anyone that you are a lady. You have already proven that to the people of this territory and most of all to me. That is all you need to do."

Laura seemed a bit perturbed at that, but I figured time would quell the situation. That's when she told me about the social at Anne Tatum's home. I didn't particularly care for Anne Tatum nor her snooty husband and she knew it. Nor did they care for me.

Laura being quite tactful, however, convinced me in her own way, that we were bound to attend. I had my reservations about having such a good time. But, what did I know? I'm only the U.S. Marshal for the Territory.

* *

The next morning brought more surprises. I stood just outside the bunkhouse with a cup of morning coffee. A couple of the boys were over at the corral saddling up the first of unbroken stock to be worked. She was a high spirited little dun filly.

Judd joined me and chuckled as he related, "Ole Mason asked the boys last night to let him help out working a wild one. They agreed. In fact, they bet a dollar a piece that he couldn't stay on any of these horses for more than ten seconds. Mason covered it. It ought to be a good show, Cole."

About that time, Mason strutted out of the bunkhouse trailed closely by the boys. It seems that Mason didn't have an outfit to match this chore, so the boys pitched in to dress him up like a true wrangler. No doubt about it, you could tell he was still a dude.

The boys grinned from ear to ear, snickering all the while. Well, they held that young filly steady until Mason climbed on board, and then they pulled the blind.

That's when all hell broke loose. That little filly reared up, stomped down, sun-fished, frog walked, and tossed her behind high into the air.

Mason gritted his teeth as he rose into the air and jarred down on the saddle—again and again and again. Laura's boys were standing around the outside of the corral, whooping it up and rooting him on.

It was, I figure, roughly eight seconds when Mason suddenly sailed into the dirt a few yards away. Wranglers rushed up to him to see if he was all right. He waved them away, walked the filly down by himself and climbed back into the saddle. I guess it was right then that he gained the respect of all of Laura's wranglers.

Mason gave a good second round but was thrown off again. This time, he was a bit rattled and sore, but nonetheless, a good sport about it. Mike Wilkes took over mounting the dun and Mason saw how it was done. The sporty filly was ridden and tamed.

Laura stood on the porch watching it all. She held a big smile on her face, and I could tell that she was trying hard not to laugh out loud.

Victoria also was by Laura's side with a look of complete shock on her face. Walter came to see the antics of his gentleman, his eyes wide with disbelief that Mason would attempt such a stunt.

The best thing about it was Mason was making friends. He was gaining some decent respect—especially when he reached into his pocket and paid off.

Laura turned to Victoria and suggested that they go for a ride. "Cousin Victoria, let's go for ride. There's a special place along the creek that borders the ranch that I'd like to show you. You and I can speak freely there."

Victoria agreed and excused herself to change into a fancy riding habit. Laura changed into her usual riding clothes. When Victoria appeared back on the porch, she eyed Laura with astonishment.

"Let's go and saddle up," announced Laura.

Victoria replied, "Saddle my own horse?"

Laura tried not to smile as she replied, "Yes, Victoria, out here, we saddle our own mounts." As an afterthought, she added, "And when the ride is over, we care for our own animals, too. We have no people to do that for us."

Although Victoria was somewhat aghast at Laura's comments, she followed her cousin to the stables where Laura brought out Mickey and told her to bring out Brandy. A sidesaddle sat on a saddletree next to Brandy's stall. Laura commenced to saddle up her mount.

Victoria was not as successful. She felt totally out of her element. She stood there with saddle and blanket in hand as Brandy maneuvered around to avoid the placement of riding gear. Laura finished with Mickey and turned to Brandy. She pushed Brandy into a good position, then fitted her with bridle, saddle blanket and saddle. "Now then," suggested Laura, "we will lead out of the stable before mounting."

Once outside, Laura helped Victoria into the sidesaddle and then mounted Mickey astride. Victoria had never ridden astride and remarked as such. "A lady does not ride astride where I come from." Laura smiled at her cousin with no other response.

Laura turned Mickey's head and led out through the gates of the Sumner Ranch. She headed north to the scenic creek that ran along her ranch property. They rode slowly while Laura pointed out the land, and landmarks, and the local creatures of nature.

Laura pointed to the distant sky, "Look, Victoria, an eagle. Isn't it graceful? Look how it floats on the air currents."

Moments later, Laura again noticed another bird of prey. "Look, a hawk, sitting on the branch of that tree to the left."

Victoria turned to look at the hawk just as Laura caught the quick flash of a wolf darting out of sight behind thick brush.

Finally, Laura reached the place that she wanted—the creek bed. The crystal water flowed lazily along the grassy embankment.

As they approached the creek, Laura pointed out that the slight splashes in the creek told of trout feeding on insects. They dismounted and Laura guided Victoria to sit with her on the bank. It was quiet and peaceful. Not a word was spoken for several minutes.

Finally, Victoria spoke, "I can see why you love it here so much. I've never seen such a place as this."

Laura thought for a moment. "That's why Jesse loved this area. He loved the West. He loved the wildness of the Territory because it is untouched by man. He became one with nature here. He cherished this land beyond all else."

Laura looked into Victoria's eyes. They were misty.

Victoria announced softly, "I would like to just sit here for a while. I revel in this peaceful setting. I am city born and city raised. I could not live here like you, but now, I understand my father's love of this country."

* *

Laura's wranglers prepared supper that evening. It was in true wrangler fashion. They basted a roast of beef on a spit for several hours. Emilita prepared side dishes that included frijoles—Mexican beans, if you will. Pans of cornbread lined the pit to bake alongside the meat. Emilita provided dishes of butter and honey to accompany cornbread.

Much to the astonishment of the Easterners, it was a good ole campfire supper, tin plates and all. Tonight, a peach cobbler from an old chuck wagon recipe topped off the meal. The guests received the full range of Western hospitality.

CHAPTER SEVEN

Victoria's Lesson

I had promised to take Victoria riding on this morning. Although not really up to it, I had given my word. I would stick to my bond.

I saddled up Warrior, and slid my Winchester rifle into the boot. Judd Ellison wisely placed a sidesaddle on Brandy figuring Victoria would ride better that way on the trail. We led the animals out of the stable to the hitching post in front of the ranch house.

Victoria stepped out on to the porch in a riding outfit sure enough suited for the East. She wore a purple riding skirt, with a white ruffled blouse and matching jacket. Her blonde hair was pinned up in a fashionable bun. Laura was nowhere to be seen. I presumed that she planned to work with her wranglers in the corrals.

"Good morning, Mr. Stockton," Victoria greeted me pleasantly. I nodded, and touching the brim of my Stetson replied, "Yes, it looks like a good day to take a ride."

Judd helped Victoria mount Brandy. I swung into the saddle and led out toward the foothills of the Rockies. We rode slowly as I pointed the signs of nature along the way.

"A pair of eagles in flight," and I pointed to the north. "Just think, they are about a quarter of a mile from us right now and in a few minutes they could be nigh into the Rockies."

Victoria nodded and mentioned, "Laura pointed out an eagle as we rode yesterday."

I pulled up short and pointed as a deer family wandered out of the trees, stopped for a few moments, and then disappeared into the wilderness again.

A mile or so later, I caught the quick flash of a coyote along our flanks. It was gone before I could mention it to my riding partner.

Victoria watched the terrain as we rode. She spotted what she described as a black and white kitten wobbling its way through the grass to our right flank. I smiled a bit and related, "Victoria, that is what we sometimes refer to as a pole cat, otherwise known as a skunk."

Well, neither of us wanted an encounter with that side of nature and held up a mite while the critter went on its way.

It was 1878. Danger was never far away in the wilds. The probability of hard-bitten bad men as well as bands of Indians roaming the wilderness followed us. Mother Nature herself frequently reared her wild side without warning as well. I spotted possible thunderstorm clouds in the distance.

Several miles out from the ranch house, we rode down into a creek bed. Brandy happened upon a rattlesnake and shied. Victoria was not in control of her. The frightened animal ran straight into the creek. She reared up and dumped Victoria into waist deep water.

I rode up beside her quickly, looked down with a sympathetic look, and offered my hand. She sputtered as she floundered in that cold water. The woman was a disheveled sight with hair matted around her face and soaked clothes. In the mean time, Brandy took off for home and her warm stable.

W-e-l-l, here we were—one horse, and as it frequently happens, a sudden thunderstorm fast upon us. There was no time to track Brandy now. We needed to find shelter from the heavy rain that was only minutes away.

I pulled the drenched Victoria up behind me. She shivered as she mounted astride and wrapped her arms around my waist. As we began to climb out of the creek bed, Warrior's ears pricked up. I stopped him quickly.

Peering over the rim of the embankment, I saw some half dozen or so fierce looking Southern Cheyenne with painted faces and feathered bonnets traveling parallel to us. Victoria stretched up a mite to follow my line of sight and saw them as well.

There is nothing like a band of painted warriors to start a woman to screaming. Before I could tell her to stay quiet, she did. I thought, "Damn, what next?"

Those warriors stopped, turned, and then started riding in our direction. I sure didn't want to shoot it out with half a dozen Cheyenne with a fidgety woman at my side.

I turned my head toward Victoria and told her, "Hang on tight! We are getting out of here."

Victoria shook with fear as she violently tightened her grip around my waist. I turned Warrior back into the creek, and with a silent prayer, headed up stream, hoping that storm would come in and cover us. It did. We rode slowly through torrents of rain, getting soaked to the bone.

In about an hour, we spotted a small cabin set back in the trees. I drew my Winchester, kicked the door open, and checked out the cabin. It appeared that the structure had been deserted for quite some time.

I helped Victoria enter the desolate building to get her out of the elements. I stabled Warrior in a dilapidated lean-to at the side of the cabin. Looking around, I pulled up a few hands full of long grass and placed them in front of Warrior. I spoke soothingly to him, "This will have to do, boy. You did good. We'll have some oats and hay when we get back to the ranch."

Once back inside the cabin, I built a small fire from kindling and some logs that lay next to the hearth. As the fire crackled its warmth, I began to shuck my clothes down to my long handles.

"I'm getting out of these wet clothes. You ought do the same."

Victoria looked at me with a "What do you think you are doing?"

I read her thoughts and offered, "You had better do the same, or you will catch your death of cold."

"I will do no such thing," she retorted. The obstinate female stood there with her hands upon her hips in complete defiance. I had just about all of Victoria that I could take.

I put on my sternest look and pointed at her. "Get those wet clothes off down to your chemise and get over by the fire to dry off or by Jove, I'll do it for you!" As she reluctantly began to disrobe, I turned away to give her some sense of privacy as best that I could in the one room cabin.

Victoria mumbled under her breath, "I'll have the law on you when we get back. A lady is not treated this way." She huffed, but complied with my instructions.

There we sat, in front of the fire. I in my long handles, and she in her chemise—each drying our clothes as best as we could. She looked a sight, and stared daggers at me the entire time.

"I never should have come out here. This land is not for a lady. I could never be like Laura—a part of the land. Now I understand why my father willed this ranch to her. She is part of the West, and I am not. I will never be part of this heathen land. I want no more of this.

When we get back to the ranch, I will call the law on you and see that you get what you deserve. Then, I will go back home—back to where there are civilized people, not the likes of you."

I pondered her statement for a long moment. "Yes, Victoria," I commented. "Laura is a woman of the West. She can ride and ride well. She can shoot a pistol or a rifle better than most men. She rides these lonely trails by herself, and knows the dangers. She is capable of handling most any situation. She is by no means a high society type, but she is a lady. Your father knew what he was doing when he willed that ranch to Laura instead of you—a self-centered prima donna."

And then, she jumped up from her seat and slapped me, before covering her face with her hands and sobbing uncontrollably. Tears flowed profusely. She continued to wipe them away with her hands and forearms without much luck. I reached up and untied my damp bandana, and then offered it to her. She stopped the sobs and looked at me. A slight smile came across her face. She nodded a bit, and uttered a choked whisper, "Thank you, sir."

* *

The storm came fast. All eyes at the Sumner Ranch nervously watched the horizon for any sign of Cole Stockton and Victoria. The first sign of the pair was when Victoria's mount, Brandy, galloped into view. The sidesaddle still in place with the reins trailing proved a sure sign of trouble.

Juan Soccorro reached Brandy first. He calmed the frightened horse, and led her to her stall for feed and a rub down. Walter and Mason were horrified. They felt certain that Victoria was lost somewhere out there in the wilderness with Cole Stockton and only one horse.

Laura turned to Walter, "Don't worry, Walter. She'll be back. There is no better man to be out there in the wilds with than Cole Stockton. By the way, Cole is a United States Marshal—the law out here, and no harm will come to her. Trust me." As Laura's wranglers repeated the assurance, the storm hit.

Streaks of lightning lit the sky. Thunder rumbled a few seconds later, and the wild wind howled fiercely. It was not fit for man nor beast in the wake of nature's fury.

The storm raged across the mountains and valleys for several hours before a brilliant rainbow arched across a clear blue sky. The sun appeared, and the air became filled with the aroma of fresh pine and wild flowers once again.

Laura changed into her everyday horse-hunting outfit of working jeans, blue denim shirt, chaps, red bandana, and black Stetson, her lucky hat.

She belted the Colt Lightning around her waist and settled it slightly low like Uncle Jesse and Cole Stockton had shown her.

Spurs jingling, she walked out of the ranch house to face Walter on the porch. Laura's boys and Mason, decked out in his newly acquired attire, sat their mounts waiting. They would ride out in search for the missing couple. Walter and Mason exchanged astonished looks at the transformed Laura.

"Walter," began Laura, "I've never been a society lady. This is how I dress to run this ranch every day. I should have remained honest to myself and let your thoughts be as they may. My boys and I will ride out across the wilds to search for Victoria and Cole. We will find them and bring them back—don't you fear."

Laura stepped from the porch, put foot to stirrup, and swung up into the saddle like she was born there. As the group trotted to the gate, a distant speck on the horizon stopped them in their tracks.

Laura Sumner and her wranglers sat silently on their mounts and watched closely as the speck grew into recognizable focus. Cole Stockton was leading Warrior with Victoria on his back.

As they drew closer, the search party could see Victoria plainly. Her riding skirt was torn and caked with mud. Her white blouse, open at the collar was streaked with mud. Her tangled hair dangled limply at her shoulders. Her powder and rouge were long gone. The woman looked very tired.

"Victoria," cried Laura, and before she could finish her sentence, Victoria interrupted her in soft voice, "Mr. Stockton and I had quite an adventure. Brandy shied at a rattlesnake and threw me into a creek. When we started to return here, we encountered a band of wild Indians. As we escaped them, the fierce storm pelted us with torrents of rain."

Victoria cleared her throat a bit before continuing, "Mr. Stockton guided us to the safety of a small cabin where we dried our clothing. When the storm broke, he ensured me of our safe return to your ranch. In the beginning, I considered calling the law on Mr. Stockton, for insulting me. He ensured our survival in the wilderness even if he hurt my feelings. I see that now."

Cole Stockton stood next to Warrior with a big grin on his face.

Walter sighed heavily and looked highly relieved with the return of his wife. "My darling, Victoria, Mr. Stockton is the law. He is the United States Marshal. His position is the major law in the Territory."

A look of surprise came across Victoria's face. "Then, it is no wonder that he was completely in charge at all times. Help me down please, Walter."

Once on the ground, Victoria faced Laura. "I have something to say, Laura. After spending time with you and experiencing this territory, I now understand completely why Father willed this ranch to you. You are part of this land just as he was. I could never live the life that you so richly embrace. We will depart back to our New York City tomorrow morning. Please convey my regrets to the ladies of the town for not attending their social."

Laura stepped forward and embraced her cousin. They stayed like that for several moments. With misty eyes and trembling lower lips, the young women had no need for conversation.

Laura smiled at Victoria, "You look a fright. I'll have my men heat up buckets of water at the fire pit so that you will have a hot bath with lavender salts." Victoria's face lit up at the thought of languishing in a tub of hot lavender water. The two women strolled arm in arm toward the house.

Judd Ellison turned to all of the wranglers. "You heard the Boss Lady! Start a good hot fire in the pit and get them buckets filled."

* *

Following breakfast the next morning, Sammy Colter stood to horse with his team in front of the house. Laura's men loaded part of the luggage in the boot and the remainder they tied down on top of the coach.

Laura and her guests stepped out of the house and gathered beside the coach. Laura and Victoria spoke quietly to one another as they shared a farewell embrace. They promised to keep in touch. Cole, Walter and Mason shook hands.

Mason turned to his new friends before boarding the coach. With handshakes all around, Mason vowed that he would return someday soon. He seemed to have found his niche in the brief time on the ranch.

Victoria was the first to board the stagecoach. She settled herself at the window and leaned out a bit. "Mr. Stockton," she called out, "thank you for your lesson about life."

Sammy Colter climbed to the high box of his coach and bit off another chaw. He looked down at his passengers and inquired if they were ready.

Momentarily came the reply from Mason, "We are situated. You may proceed, driver."

With a loud voice, Sammy advised, "Hold on to your hats! We going to leave in a whirlwind of horseflesh and dust!"

Then, with a big toothy grin on his whiskered face, he winked at Laura. He cracked his whip into the air above his animals and shouted the words that set the six-horse team leaning into their harnesses.

The Overland coach lurched forward. The visitors waved from the windows as the coach rumbled and swayed. It grew smaller and smaller in the distance.

Cole stood beside Laura, his arm around her waist. He drew her close and looked down into those crystal blue eyes. "Welcome back. You sure are pretty for a lady horse rancher," he whispered in her ear. Laura snuggled closer to him.

Cole gently put his arms around her and pulled her to him. Laura looked deeply into his eyes, and relaxed against him. He gently lifted her face to his and kissed her fully amongst the silent grins of the wrangler crowd.

Cole Stockton learned later that the Wooley brothers stayed on at the Widow Hooper's place at her suggestion. She soon had one of the best farms in the territory. It's surprising how a good hearted woman with a knack for good cooking can bring out the best in a man, or men.

CHAPTER EIGHT

Trouble in Dallas

Carroll and Mary Sumner stood on the porch of their small farmhouse listening to the stocky man sitting in the single horse buggy.

"You can't say that I didn't warn you before Sumner. Your note is more than ninety days overdue at my bank. I'm sorry to let you know that I had to sell the note to Charles Farnum in order to protect the interest of the bank. You will have to deal with him now."

Martin Duncan, the Dallas bank president, cleared his throat a moment before continuing. "By the terms of the mortgage sale, you have ninety days to pay the entire note of two thousand dollars to Farnum or he can foreclose. Take my advice, Sumner and move out. Farnum is known for hard dealings. I know that he wants this land to gain control of the water rights. He runs too many cattle for his own range. To survive, he needs additional land and most of all—water. You know he carries some hard gunmen on his payroll."

Carroll replied, "Yes, Mr. Duncan. We understand. But, two thousand dollars might as well be a hundred times that amount. We don't have it. With the drought these last three years, we have just been able to feed ourselves, the stock, and buy some seed for planting. There is no more money. I sure wish that you had extended our loans. We have worked hard for this land over the past twenty-five years and we won't let it go without a fight."

"Yes, Sumner. I thought that you might. That's why I'm warning you. Leave with your lives. The land ain't worth dying over."

Mary Sumner interjected with steadfast determination. "You got that wrong, Mr. Duncan. Our land is worth dying over. This is our home. No one is going to take our land. Not you, not Farnum, no one! We have worked too hard for it."

"You Sumners are stubborn, like all the rest. Suit yourselves. I tried to warn you." The banker shook his head, gathered up the reins and spoke to his dapple gray mare. The buggy turned and they trotted out of sight.

Mary Sumner turned to her husband. "Carroll, we've got to send a message to Laura. I know we've spoken about this before, but maybe, just maybe, Laura can help out some. In her last letter, she mentioned selling a great number of horses. Maybe she can provide enough money to stall this situation with Mr. Farnum. I just know that she would want to help. All we have to do is tell her."

Carroll responded with, "Alright, Mary. I can't think of anything else to do. We'll send a wire to Laura. A letter can't get there in time to help much."

* *

Laura Sumner made her way across the ranch yard to the corral. Lady, her puppy of six months, ran along side of her. Every so often, the golden-haired ball of fur would stop, sniff the ground and then exuberantly run all around Laura, her tail wagging like a whip.

Judd Ellison, Laura's foreman, along with wranglers Juan and Mike leaned against the bars of the main corral watching the newest stock.

"Good morning, boys," Laura greeted. "Well, Judd, how do they look?"

"Morning, Miss Laura. You sure got a good deal when you bought these horses from that old wild horse wrangler. I've known Jim Clark for some ten years now, and he is good at his trade. I tried to talk him into joining us a time back, but he declined. He's a loner. He likes the freedom to do as he pleases."

Laura nodded and responded, "Does that mean that you can't do what you please, Judd?"

"Miss Laura. Don't do that to me. You know what I mean. You know that we value working with you. There is no other person we would want to work for, especially come holiday season. You cook up the best all-out ranch feast we ever ate."

Laura blushed a bit. Juan Soccorro turned to Laura. "Senorita Laura. I must speak to you alone for a moment."

Laura nodded and beckoned Juan to follow her to the end of the corrals. "What is it Juan? Is there something wrong?"

"I donno," related Juan, "Something must be terribly wrong with Emilita. She seems weary and wistful every morning. She is becoming sharp with me—for no reason. I don't know what I can do to please her. I've tried to talk to her, but she won't answer me. Would you speak to her to try to find out what is wrong? I want to understand and help her with whatever is on her mind."

Laura smiled. "Yes, Juan. I will speak with Emilita. I am sure that everything will be all right. She might even surprise you."

Just then, a rider galloped into the ranch yard and up to the corral. Laura and her wranglers turned to greet Tommy Wagner, the telegraph runner.

"Good morning, Miss Laura. We got a telegram for you this morning and seeing as it is marked urgent, Mr. Wilson sent me out here with it."

"Thank you, Tommy. Say, have you had your breakfast yet?"

"No Ma'am! I've eaten nothing since last night."

"O.K., Tommy, ride over to the house and ask Emilita to fix you up a plate of huevos rancheros. Have some of that fresh milk, too. A growing boy like you needs to drink a lot of milk."

Tommy blushed. He really liked Laura Sumner and thought her one of the most beautiful women in all of the Lower Colorado. He especially enjoyed any occasion to visit the Sumner Ranch. Laura usually had cookies, or cinnamon rolls, a cake, or some type of pie on hand. Appreciative and knowing how young men liked baked goods, Laura always afforded Tommy something extra for his ride.

Laura opened the telegram and read it silently. Judd watched her expression as she read. Her eyes went wide. He observed a look of disbelief, and then, one of angry determination.

"Something wrong, Boss?" queried Judd. "Can we help?"

"Judd, I've got to go to Texas for a while. My parents are in some sort of difficulty and I'm going to help them as much as possible. I shouldn't be gone over a month. Once again, you'll have to take over for me. I trust you, Judd. You've always come through for me."

"Shucks, Miss Laura. The boys and I are glad to keep this here ranch going. It's our home, too! You go ahead and do what you have to do. We will see things through. You can bet on it."

"Oh! One other thing, Judd. Cole Stockton is out there on the trails somewhere. I am leaving on the next stage, this very afternoon. When he gets back, tell him where I've gone and why. Tell him I will be back just as soon as all is well."

"I'll tell him, Miss Laura. Don't you fret none."

Chapter Nine

Outlaws in the Wilderness

In utter silence, Cole Stockton moved slowly through the thick brush, Winchester at the ready. He had tracked three wanted men for at least a hundred miles through all manner of terrain. Now, they were within fifty yards of him. The morning air held the aroma of bacon frying, biscuits baking, and coffee boiling. The men were about to eat their breakfast, unaware of his presence.

Sid Mayer, Red Tulley, and Kid Larson sat around the campfire wolfing down their meager fare when a crackle resounded to their left. Each man dropped his plate, jumped to his feet, and drew his weapon.

Anxiety showed on each man's face. Nervous eyes flitted along the thickets. Ears strained to pick up the slightest sound. There was stillness and quiet. Then, another faint crackle floated through the still morning. The trio cocked their weapons.

"Who's there? Come out or get filled with lead," Sid Mayer challenged.

A long silence prevailed before all hell broke loose. A low growl followed by a fierce moan, and then a huge silver-tipped grizzly bounded into their camp. Its jaws were wide open with fangs bared. Saliva frothed from its mouth.

"Holy Mother of God!" screamed Red in fear. "A mad grizzly!"

Each man fired a round, but in their haste, they jerked the trigger instead of squeezing it. All three bullets missed the charging bear. In panic, weapons dropped as they scattered to the nearest trees. They climbed as high and as fast as they could.

Red Tulley gazed down while climbing the tree that he reached. The grizzly was full height on his hind legs clawing the tree bark just inches below his boots. The powerful bear began clambering up after him. Red screamed in terror. His two partners yelled at him to climb faster. His heavy frame hindered a more rapid climb.

The bear continued to labor up the tree with jaws open wide. Red felt the searing pain as sharp fangs closed down on his right ankle. Fear claimed his body as he screamed in pain.

The din was suddenly shattered by the sharp crack of a rifle. The grizzly jerked upon the impact of the heavy lead. The animal roared out in anguish, yet held Red in his vice grip. Another slug slammed into the bear before it opened its mouth releasing the ankle with an piercing growl. The enormous bear dropped to the ground, floundering in pain and rage. He turned to face this new adversary.

A stranger stepped into the campsite and faced the beast. He quickly leveled another round into the chamber of his Winchester before he lined the muzzle straight into the face of the grizzly and waited.

The giant bear rose on his hind legs, powerfully upraised for a deadly strike. His massive jaws gaped wide open. The grizzly lumbered forward toward the intruder, forelegs raised with deadly razor sharp claws open for the attack.

As the bear rumbled toward the lone rifleman, flame and hot lead spit three times in rapid succession from the bore of the Winchester. All three shots slammed into the grizzly's mouth, exiting through the back of its skull. The massive hulk fell dead with a heavy thud a mere six feet in front of United States Marshal Cole Stockton.

Stockton levered another round into the chamber of the rifle and stood with the butt of the rifle on his hip. He addressed the three fugitives. "Morning, boys, U.S. Marshal. I guess you might say that I've got ya'll treed. Come on down, real easy now and no one will get hurt."

The three outlaws slowly slid down from their perches. Red Tulley's leg was bleeding profusely from the calf down to his ankle. He screamed in pain.

"Red, I'll take care of you in a minute. All of you shuck your gun belts or take lead."

With no decision to make, all three gun belts slipped to the ground before hands raised high into the air. They were had, fair and square, and accepted it.

Stockton moved to the Kid, turned him around and cuffed his hands behind his back. Next, the lawman approached Sid and did likewise. Finally, he had Red lie on the ground, his hands over his head on either side of a sapling. He cuffed him around the tree.

"Well, now. You are all under arrest for several charges, including theft."

"Yah, Marshal, we're innocent! We didn't steal no horses, we didn't steal no cows, and we sure enough did not burn down no barns. So, what do you have to say about that?"

"I'd say that you described the warrant pretty well," retorted Stockton.

Red Tulley blurted out in a quivering voice, "Marshal Stockton! Damn it! My leg is bleeding something fierce. You got to do something fast."

"Alright, Red, where's your saddle bags?"

"What do you want my saddlebags for, Marshal?"

"Well, now, Red. You don't think that I'm going to bandage up your bleeding leg with my extra shirt do you? It's your leg, and your shirt for the dressing."

Red moaned as he pointed out his gear. Stockton rummaged the saddlebags and found a wadded up shirt. Using his belt knife, he cut it into a large wound dressing, then, further sliced it into bandage strips. He moved to Red and tore open his pants leg to reveal the wound.

After pouring water from a canteen over the wound, Stockton further rummaged the remainder of the trio's gear until he found what he was looking for. He took the small bottle of whiskey and poured some over Red's ankle to sterilize it. Then, he bandaged the ankle.

A bit later, three sullen prisoners sat around their campfire watching Cole Stockton eat up the remnants of _their_ bacon, _their_ biscuits, and drink up _their_ coffee.

"Thanks for the grub, boys. I think I earned it. After all, none of you kilt that grizzly. A man gets mighty hungry after a chore like that."

After cleaning up the breakfast plates, tin cups, and utensils, the wily marshal had Sid Mayer and Kid Larsen stand up while he removed the cuffs from each, one at a time, and re-cuff their hands in front of them. He then had them break camp and saddle up their mounts.

Mayer and Larsen helped Red Tulley up on his horse. Then, they mounted their animals. Stockton strung a rope between each of the three animals and led them out of camp through the thickets to where his chestnut stallion Warrior waited.

"All right, boys, ride easy in the saddle. It's a few days of travel back to Denver. Let's make it an uneventful trip."

CHAPTER TEN

The Road to Dallas

Laura Sumner packed two valise bags for the trip to Texas before she dressed in one of her best traveling dresses. She looked quite the lady. Looking in the mirror, Laura thought, "I wonder what Victoria and Walter would think of my attire today."

When she was ready, Emilita helped her carry her belongings out to the porch.

"Emilita, let's have a cup of tea," announced Laura with a soft smile on her face. The two women sat across the small table in the kitchen from each other as they conversed in soft tones.

"Juan asked me to speak with you. He is concerned that there might be something bothering you. He wants to help you, if he can."

The young woman responded, "There is nothing wrong, but I have been a little queasy in the stomach every morning now. I have just felt a bit sick. It will pass. I am sorry for Juan, though. I know that I have been sharp with him. I will try to be more pleasant."

Laura smiled at her, "Emilita, I want you to go to town with us to see Doctor Simmons. I think that you are in for a very wonderful surprise. I think that you are going to have a baby."

Emilita's mouth dropped wide open and her eyes lit up with a strange wonderment. "A baby?"

"Yes, Emilita. I think that you are with child. Don't tell Juan until Doctor Simmons confirms it. Then, you can surprise him."

Laura saw a glowing expression come over Emilita's face. The young woman sighed with an aura of absolute love and endearment.

* *

Two hours later, Juan Soccorro reined back on the team pulling the ranch wagon. He leaped out of the seat to tie the reins around the hitching rack, then stepped to the side of the wagon to help Laura Sumner down. Then he lifted Emilita down from the wagon. Juan did not understand why Miss Laura had his wife brought along to town.

"Juan. Take Emilita over to Doctor Simmons' office. You can wait there for her. I think that you will be in for a very wonderful surprise."

Laura watched as the young couple walked hand in hand down the boardwalk to the doctor's office. She smiled with a knowing look as a slight mist filled her eyes.

* *

Laura turned heads in a navy two-piece traveling dress with white ruffled blouse. She wore an ivory broach at the neck and a bright blue ribbon around her dark hair, letting it fall down over her shoulders.

The ranch woman's luggage consisted of two valises and a leather handbag. The large valise would be put in the boot or on top of the stagecoach. She kept the smaller valise with her inside the coach. Amongst personal items, it held her gunbelt and Colt .38 Lightning revolver.

Laura thought, "I guess that I've been around Cole Stockton too long. I'm taking my revolver everywhere that I go."

Laura turned suddenly, when she heard the loud voice behind her. "Glory be! Miss Laura, is that you? My, you look like a fine lady this morning."

Laura smiled. "Sammy Colter! Now, don't tell me that you're driving the coach down toward Texas this trip."

"You got that right, Laura. Is that where you are headed? By God, I'll trade some runs along the way and see you personally to your destination. This ole coach line owes me some time to myself anyways."

"I'd be proud to have you accompany me, Sammy."

"Well now," related Sammy. "We'll just have to have you ride up on the high box sometime during the trip."

Laura flushed with Sammy's last comment. To ride up on the high box on the seat of the driver and shotgun guard was an honor bestowed only to the most respected of passengers. Laura was enthralled. She had ridden several coaches before, but never up on the high box.

It was just before the coach boarding time when a wildly excited Juan Soccorro, with his Emilita trailing, came down the boardwalk. They waved to Laura.

"Senorita Laura! Senorita Laura!" cried a proud Juan. "Un momento! We have something to tell you!" The couple met with Laura to the side of the stagecoach station. Juan smiled from ear to ear as he related, "We are going to have a baby." Emilita stood demurely beaming. The young couple was jubilant.

Laura exhibited bright eyes and a wide smile for the two of them, "See, Juan, I told you that you would get a surprise. You can take Emilita home now. I won't need you. The coach is almost ready to board. You be very careful on the way back to the ranch."

"Si, Miss Laura. I will be very careful."

Thirty minutes later, Sammy Colter spoke lovingly to his team and they surged forward into the harness and traces. "Ya-hoo! Come on youse Cayuses. Stretch out! Come on Bessie, come on Dingus, get up there Baldy. Come on now, roll this ole coach down that road. Hee-Haw."

Laura sat beside an older woman traveling through Colorado. She jerked and swayed with the rocking of the coach, as did Laura. The seat across from them was taken by a young couple who appeared to be recently married. It was evident that they had not traveled by stagecoach before. They held on to one another, but failed to sway with the coach. The other man in the coach held a somber face with a beard. He wore his Colt Army .45 in a cross draw fashion. His eyes were cold.

The trip down through the New Mexico Territory proved uneventful. The somber man got off at Las Vegas, New Mexico. He was replaced by a thin, frail woman. Her modest dress gave the appearance of a farm woman. The coach continued southeast, crossing into Texas. The newlywed couple left them at Abilene, and two rough men took their seats.

The first of these men appeared to be in his early thirties while the other in his late forties. Both men had bushy mustaches and wore their guns tied down. One chewed tobacco and continually spat out the window. The other merely folded his burly arms across his massive chest and napped with an occasional snort.

When Laura read their eyes, a quick shiver ran down her spine. She didn't like the looks of these two. She visited pleasantly with the older woman who still rode beside her.

Much to her liking, both of the unpleasant men disembarked at Fort Belknap. The older lady stayed with the coach until Dallas with Laura.

On the final leg of the trip Sammy Colter insisted that Laura ride up on the high box to "make your arrival with flourish and excitement."

Laura loved the rush of wind to her face. She enjoyed the excitement of being up high and watching the horses as they stretched out into the traces. Sammy whistled a merry tune as they neared the outskirts of Dallas. Just as they entered the city, Sammy yelled out a warning to Laura.

"Hang on Laura! Here we go! Sammy slapped the reins to the team's back. H-e-e H-a-w! Come on youse rangy mustangs. Lean into that harness! Come on now, before I sell ya'll to farmers for plow horses."

The Overland Stage with Sammy Colter in the driver's seat thundered into Dallas, Texas and slid to a dust-swirling halt directly in front of the express office. The station agent ran out of the office shouting at Sammy.

"Dammit, Colter! I've told you before about these hoo-rah arrivals. By the way, what's a woman doing up in the shotgun's seat? There are rules about that."

"Yer absolutely correct," retorted Sammy, "and, whoever I want up here will ride here. Stuff that in yer shirt, John."

The station agent gritted his teeth and shook his fist at Sammy.

"You just watch it, Colter!"

Sammy winked at Laura. She could hardly contain her giggle. Yes, Sammy was quite a character. He was a crusty old man, but he was one of the best friends that a person could have. She loved his candidness.

Laura suddenly looked down upon her mother and father. They had received her wire and were waiting on the station platform for the stage to arrive.

Mary Sumner was somewhat awestruck that Laura would even consider riding up in the high box of a stagecoach. It was so very high up, not to mention windy and dusty. But, that was Laura up there. Laura loved an adventure. Her father looked upon her with soft eyes. It was good to see his daughter again.

The station agent helped Laura down from the high box. Once on the ground, she turned and rushed into her parents' wide opened arms. The family held each other close for a long time.

After retrieving her luggage, Laura and her parents walked to the waiting farm wagon. They had just climbed aboard and settled themselves when several riders turned the street corner and stopped before them.

The leader was Charles Farnum with five gunhands at his side. Farnum sat his horse and glared at Carroll Sumner for a long moment. Finally, he spoke with the voice of authority. "Sumner. I want you off that farm within thirty days. You don't go, I will send my man Chase Logan there, to move you his way. He ain't gentle about it."

Laura had heard that name before. Chase Logan was a hired killer. Word had it that he was fast with a gun, extremely vicious, and loved to victimize his quarry before he killed them. Laura glared with firmness at Logan. She could feel the icy stare of death upon her. She momentarily averted her eyes. Logan grinned crookedly.

"Yah, lady, I got the look, ain't I? You've heard of me before. I can tell it in your eyes. Maybe you and I will get real close before this is all over."

Laura retorted, "I think not, Mr. Logan. I have a certain friend already who doesn't cotton to the likes of you."

Chase Logan laughed with a wicked sneer. "Bring him along. I will be glad to take care of him, too."

Laura thought for a split second before replying to Logan. She stared directly into his dark eyes with a determined response. "You know, Mr. Logan, I might just ask him to come to Dallas. I think that you should meet my friend. I know that you two will understand each other very well."

Logan laughed out loud, "Yah, I'd like to meet the lily-livered gent that would be close to a fine spirited woman like you."

Laura Sumner smiled and thought, "I'd like to see you say that to Cole Stockton's face."

Charles Farnum interrupted further discussion. "You see to it that you are off that land in thirty days, or else." The rancher and his riders shoved on past the ranch wagon and rode toward the saloon section of town.

Carroll and Mary Sumner turned to Laura and shook their heads. They now had a spark of regret at involving their precious daughter in the midst of this land war.

"Laura," said her father quietly, "perhaps it would be better if you just took the next stage back to Colorado. We will work this out ourselves."

Laura's reply was quick, "Nonsense, Father. I see what you're up against. I'm here now. I'm going to help you keep the farm. Don't argue with me. You know how stubborn I am. Besides, that Logan guy got my dander up. In fact, I think that I will wire my very close friend, asking that he travel here to assist. He knows how to handle situations of this sort. I must let you know, Mother and Father, that this man is very special to me. Perhaps it is time that you met him. Yes, let's stop by the telegraph office on the way home."

Mary Sumner saw the love in her daughter's eyes as she spoke of this special friend. She could sense the devotion that Laura held for this man. She would talk with Laura about it soon. She wanted to know everything about the man who could make Laura's eyes shine like that.

* *

Later in the afternoon, after arriving at the Sumner farm, Mary Sumner and her beloved daughter were alone in Laura's old room. The women unpacked Laura's belongings.

"Laura, Dear. Tell me all about this special friend of yours; the one you sent the telegram to. I saw a distinct light in your eyes. It was the shining that tells me that you are in love. Is it true?"

"Mother, you always did know when things made me happy or sad. Yes. I am in love. My friend is, well, very special to me. We have been through a lot together. We haven't married, although he has asked me—at least once. Actually, the thought is very present within both of us, but it can't happen—not just yet."

Laura hesitated a long moment. "My friend, please understand this, holds a very important job and to marry would only hinder his position. He is very good at what he does, and men like him are sorely needed in the West. You will know what I mean when he arrives."

Mary Sumner smiled lovingly at her daughter, "Well, is he a banker, a lawyer, or a general storekeeper? Perhaps he is an important Judge."

Laura grinned a bit. "W-e-l-l, Mother, you won't tell Father. He deals in justice."

Mary's eyes widened, "Oh, then he practices law."

To which Laura replied, "You might say that. I would prefer you to meet him before I say any more. I can say that his presence and encouragement have helped me to build my dreams more than any other influence. No matter what the situation, he stands by my side and supports me in my efforts."

"Tell me more, Laura. What does he look like?"

"Well, Mother, he is a bit older than I. Tall and lanky with soft, yet strong hands. His face is tanned from the sun and wind from the trails he rides. He has piercing blue-green eyes that look into your very soul. Day to day he dresses in a dark suit with light blue or white shirt, string tie, and dark Stetson. When out on the trails, he wears old faded jeans, a dark blue shirt, bandana, an old dark coat and dark Stetson."

Laura took a deep breath before continuing, "He is clean shaven most of the time. Most of all, when the chips are down, he gets this silly grin on his face that resembles a little boy caught with his hand in the cookie jar. He is gentle with me, and to tell you the truth, Mother, just looking into his eyes gives me a sense of serenity. Yes, I am in love with this man."

Mary Sumner had tears in her eyes as she held her daughter's gaze. "My dear, Laura. I can tell. Just now, watching your face as you spoke of your special friend, your eyes were shining with a brilliance that I have never before seen. I also felt warmth radiating from you. It is a warmth that speaks of an eternal bond. I can hardly wait to meet this special friend of yours."

"I hope that you and Father will like him, Mother. I know that he will help us save this farm. That greedy rancher Farnum and his riders have a big surprise coming. They just don't know what they are up against."

Mary hung her head. When she raised her face to her daughter, she whispered hoarsely, "Laura, I am worried about your father. You know that he will fight for this land. We have put too many years of toil and love into this soil to have it taken from us because of hard luck and greedy people. I fear that man, Chase Logan. I fear that he will hound us until your father makes a mistake, then—I hate to think of the consequences. Your father is older now and has not had a gun in his hand in several years. There was no need to, up until now. Your father wears his pistol every day now."

Laura took Mary's hands in hers. "Mother, we must convince Father to take off that gun and always be unarmed. He must never lend himself to be goaded into touching a weapon. You may be taken with this, but I brought my gunbelt. Yes, Mother, don't look so surprised. Up in the wilds of Colorado, I wear it every day. I know how to use mine because I was taught by the best. I will wear the gun and I will deal with those men. Rest assured that I can handle the situation."

Laura turned to her valise, opened it, and took out her tooled gunbelt and Colt Lightning Revolver. She placed it on the bed.

"Mother, I am going to change into my everyday working clothes. Please don't be alarmed. I may not look like a lady, but this who I am when I run my ranch."

Mary Sumner stood to look directly at her daughter. With a sigh, she responded, "My dear, Laura. The character of a lady is within, not on the outside. I do hope that you will wear a dress for the party, though."

Laura was taken back. "A party?"

"Yes, Laura. We want to have a welcome home party for you. I am thinking about Saturday next week. I want to invite some of your old friends for dinner, cake and coffee. By the way, Jeffrey Marlowe is still around. He divorced that woman. His horse ranch is thriving. He asks about you every so often. I tell him only that you are happy where you are. I believe that he regrets how he treated you. Will you be too unhappy should I ask him to come to the party?"

Laura thought for a long moment. "I have forgiven and forgotten now, Mother. I have seen my destiny. Yes. You may invite him. And— yes, I will dress like a lady, just for you."

Mary Sumner embraced her daughter. Laura was a real lady.

* *

Charles Farnum and Chase Logan sat at a table toward the rear of the saloon conversing in hushed tones when two hard drifters entered the batwing doors and ambled up to the bar. Chase grinned at Farnum.

"Mr. Farnum, my two friends are here. Let me introduce you." Chase rose from his chair and walked to the bar. "Strahan! Pender! You got here in good time. You two come on over to my table. Bring that bottle with you. The drinks are on the boss."

The three men shook hands. Jake Pender grabbed up their bottle of whiskey. The three made their way to the table in the rear to join Charles Farnum.

"Mr. Farnum, I'd like you to meet Bob Strahan and Jake Pender, two good men. We've done business together up around Santa Fe, and El Paso. Their work is final. None of them sod busters will dare to stay on their lands after we get through with them. You will have all the range and all the water that you need to run your herds. Payment is, of course, as we discussed. Two thousand each, half now and half when the job is complete. We will start with that Sumner farm."

Charles Farnum grinned wickedly, as he nodded his head with authority. He would not wait until the end of the mortgage sale terms. He would run Sumner off his land by the end of the month. After all, suppose the old man got riled up and drew a gun? His men would be forced to defend themselves. It would be self defense and the widow would fear for her own safety and leave.

Suddenly, a thought ran through Farnum's mind. "Who was that woman in the wagon with the Sumners? What is her stake in this?" The thought bothered him and he didn't know why.

Chase Logan also thought of that young woman. He recalled how she curtly responded to his comments with fire and venom. She was a real looker all right. She was some kind of woman. She knew how to look after herself very well.

Logan smiled, thinking of his prowess with women. He had his way with women in the past. He would have his way with this woman before this show was over. He continued to think of Laura. Her composure in the face of men of violent experience was alarming. This woman could read men. She knew him for what he was—a man of vengence.

Logan continued to relive his encounter with Laura. She mentioned her special friend. This was a woman sure of her ability. Most women like her had men who bowed to their wishes or had no men at all. More than likely, her friend was some fancy who never packed a gun. He probably sang in the church choir and wore tailored suits. Logan smirked at the image he had of this woman's friend.

He mused, "I hope that she does send for this friend. I'd like nothing better than to teach him the law of the West, where men know how to carry a gun and are prepared to use it. I'll show him. And, then, I'll teach that young woman to mind her manners around me."

The four men drank to the task before them and sealed their bond. Within the next two weeks the horror of a land war would begin and nothing would stand in their way.

CHAPTER ELEVEN

An Urgent Message

Cole Stockton sat in a wooden swivel chair at the jail. He sipped hot coffee and swapped stories with Sheriff J.C. Kincaid.

"Your coffee is getting better, J.C. I take it that you don't lace it with gunpowder anymore. It does have distinct flavor. I can't put my finger on it, but I've tasted it before."

"Well, Cole. I was jawing with Mrs. Kalady the other day. You know her. She likes to bake, so she sells her extras down at the general store. Anyway, she told me to put nutmeg in the coffee grounds. It sure gives it kind of a nutty flavor, doesn't it?"

"J.C., why don't you just grind up the regular coffee beans and leave it at that. I mean, coffee is coffee and it tastes just fine without anything in it. If you really want flavor, just add more beans. That's the way I like it."

Just then, Tommy Walker, the telegraph runner appeared. "Howdy, Sheriff Kincaid. Hello to you, Marshal Stockton." And, then, looking directly at Cole, he continued, "I knew that you were here, I saw Warrior out front. Anyways, we got this here telegram just in from Miss Laura. She's in Dallas, you know, and it looks like she wants you to come on down there and help out with some kind of situation."

Sheriff Kincaid lowered his head a bit to look directly at the youth as he inquired, "Tommy, do you read every telegram that comes in?"

"Oh, no, Sir. I only read the most interesting ones. After all, I am learning to operate the telegraph keys and one day, I will be a full-fledged operator."

Cole took the telegram from Tommy's hand and read it silently.

PRIORITY: URGENT
TO: COLE STOCKTON, US MARSHAL, LOWER COLORADO TERR.

PROBLEM ONLY YOU CAN HANDLE. COME TO DALLAS.

PLEASE ADVISE. LAURA

Cole turned to Sheriff Kincaid, "J.C., there must be some kind of bad trouble there in Dallas. Laura wouldn't send a wire like this unless it involved possible gunplay in some fashion. I'm riding there as soon as I can make ready."

He turned to the telegraph runner, "Tommy, send a wire back. Send only that I am coming. Mark that message for Laura Sumner and her alone."

Tommy dashed out the door. Cole pondered the wire once again, and remarked to his friend, "You know, J.C., if this is the kind of trouble I think it is, I might need a hand. I have some friends in Texas and I think that they might like to get involved in helping Laura as well. I'll send another wire before I leave town."

Cole chatted with J.C. Kincaid a bit longer. Then, he rode back to Laura Sumner's ranch. He packed his travel gear, and mounted Warrior. As a last minute thought, he rode over to the stables to saddle up Mickey.

As he approached the black, he said softly, "Hi, Mickey. I'll bet that you have missed Laura lately. Let's go down there to Dallas and surprise her. I know that she'll be glad to see you." Mickey shook his head up and down as though he understood.

Cole met Judd Ellison, Laura's foreman, as he led Mickey out of the barn. "Going to Dallas, Cole?" Cole replied affirmatively, "Yes, Judd. I figure that it will take me about ten to twelve hard days travel to make the trip. I've got places in mind to stop and rest along the way, but it's the most direct route."

A half hour later, Cole Stockton was riding out on Warrior and leading Mickey toward the passes into the New Mexico Territory, and further on into Texas, his homeland.

* *

Suppertime this evening at Penny Cooper's Boarding House meant the aroma of roasted wild turkey, freshly baked bread, and coffee floated on the air. A juicy wild berry cobbler cooled on the sideboard for dessert. Boarders and regulars alike shuffled to their accustomed seats at the long table.

As with all boarding houses, serving platters and bowls passed down the line, making a complete round of the table.

Justin Cooper, Penny's husband, carved the turkey. Each boarder received a portion to their liking. Finally, he sat down to his own plate, piled high. Penny was a good cook and Coop seemed to have gained a good twenty pounds since he retired from the Texas Rangers.

Everyone was busy visiting and enjoying the delicious meal when the small bell on the parlor door tinkled. The door closed and footsteps scurried into the dining area. Penny Cooper turned her eyes toward the archway. Johnny Tindall, the telegraph runner, was out of breath from his run to Penny's Boarding House.

"I got a wire here for Coop!" he exclaimed. "It's from Cole Stockton— the gunfighter."

Penny Ann Cooper's eyes suddenly lit up with the brilliance of a thousand stars on a clear Texas night. "Cole Stockton!" she said the name loudly. Justin Cooper stood up and quickly moved to Penny's side, as did Coop's two partners, Josh Slater and Jim Farley.

The former Texas Rangers, now working as range detectives, leaned in toward Coop. What is up? Cole Stockton just doesn't send wires off the cuff. There must be something BIG going on. Let's have it. We're all ears."

"Well, boys, Cole doesn't say much. He just says *Dallas. St. Charles Hotel. Need help.*" Coop pondered the telegram only a moment before relating, "I highly suspect that there could be gunplay and lots of it. But, when Cole Stockton needs help, we are the ones to go."

Justin Cooper looked at his partners, Slater and Farley. Both nodded their heads in unison. "We'll be ready at first light."

A lively party of three rode out of Fort Stockton early the next morning. Penny Cooper had risen early and fixed her husband and his best friends a good breakfast for the trail. She also put together a bait of biscuits, dried beef strips, ham slices, and cheese for each man.

Penny smiled and waved as the trio of Ranger friends rode toward Dallas. They were like young cavaliers going on a quest.

Chapter Twelve

Old Acquaintances

A week later, Saturday evening brought guests to the Sumner farm. Carroll Sumner spent the day setting up two long picnic tables and a plank dance floor. Mary and Laura baked and decorated a cake, and made two apple pies before preparing a picnic party of fried chicken with all the trimmings. There was a berry punch. Naturally, Laura made a pot of freshly ground coffee.

The guests included a number of Laura's friends from her teen years. Many had spouses now who accompanied them. Laura greeted each and every one with stimulating conversation. Friends spoke of their dreams and accomplishments. They shared stories of how they met their spouses, and of their children. Her friends were amazed to hear Laura relate her quest to have the best horse ranch in the Colorado Territory. She related some of her wild horse hunting and wrangling adventures.

This childhood friend, now a beautiful young woman, was courageous, yes, even bold enough to come head on with Indians and horse thieves. And, she was boss lady to horse wranglers.

Laura's closest girl friends saw her bare ring finger which led them to ask about a special fellow and marriage. "I've not been married," she told them, "however, I do have a very special friend."

At their insistence, she told them of Cole Stockton, using his Christian names Bob Cole. She consciously refrained from divulging information that she knew would cause eyebrows to raise in wonder and bewilderment. She did bring wide-eyed envy among the women with her description of Cole and his support of her dreams. Oh, yes, he traveled a lot in his business.

Laura was in the midst of relating comments about her special friend when Jeffery Marlowe arrived. In his usual style, he rode a thoroughbred stallion. The dark mane and tail, with white star on his forehead, complimented his steel gray color.

Laura's once intended, Jeffrey, dismounted and turned to see Laura with other young women on the lawn. Their eyes met. He seemed much older now. The luster that once gleamed was gone. As in the past, he dressed as a gentleman, with starched white shirt, dark suit, and navy tie. His well polished boots reached almost to his knees.

Laura was breathtakingly beautiful. She wore a navy blue skirt and vest with pale blue blouse. At her neck, she wore a navy velvet ribbon that held a silver star medallion that Cole Stockton had given her. Her long dark hair cascaded over her shoulders and was held in place with another blue ribbon.

The group of young women stepped back to allow Jeffrey to join their circle. Each kept her eyes on Laura to see her reaction to her ex-fiancé. Did Laura know he was coming?

In awe, Jeffrey stepped up to Laura, bowed slightly, and held out his hands to her. She laid her hands in his and looked deep into his eyes with a smile.

"How very nice to see you again, Laura. You look absolutely wonderful. Words cannot express my gratitude at being invited to this reception."

"It's nice to see you, too, Jeffrey. Thank you for joining us this evening. We'll need to catch up on our lives, especially life with our horses. Father told me that your dreams of a thoroughbred horse ranch have come true and that you have some of the most coveted horses in Texas. I'm happy for you. Please come and join the party."

Laura saw the spark of infatuation in Jeffrey's eyes rekindling, and her heart thumped a bit. Even though he broke her heart once, she found that she held more than a fondness for him. She wondered for a moment if it were wishful pangs of love, or merely his good looks, success, and fond memories of a time past. She looked once again into Jeffrey's eyes. Yes, he still loved her.

After supper and dessert, several of the neighbors broke out their fiddles and guitars. They played some of Laura's favorite songs. Jeffrey was the first to ask Laura to dance. She accepted graciously and immediately they were gliding flawlessly across the crude plank dance floor as though time, a broken heart, and separation had never occurred.

Memories of old times flashed through Laura's mind. She had forgotten how well Jeffrey danced. The smile on her face showed that she was having fun. The couple chatted pleasantries as they danced.

Jeffrey danced most of the selections with Laura. She was radiant. As guests were leaving, Jeffrey turned to Laura and asked, "My dear Laura. Would you do me the honor of riding with me tomorrow morning? I will bring one of my prize horses for you to ride."

Laura reflected on this invitation for only a moment, then replied, "Yes, Jeffrey. I will go riding with you tomorrow morning. I'll be ready at eight o'clock."

Jeffrey smiled and took her hands in his. He held them very gently. He looked down at her and spoke softly, "Thank you, Laura."

Laura watched him as he turned to his horse, mounted, and rode away toward his ranch. Laura stood there transfixed for a while. Mary Sumner observed Laura from the table that she was clearing and came to Laura. She placed her arm around her daughter's waist.

"My dear, I think that he still has strong feelings for you."

"Yes, Mother. He does. He asked me to go riding with him in the morning."

"And, what did you say, dear?"

"I accepted. I don't know why, but I feel that I must do this. I once loved him with all my heart, Mother, and tonight I felt a strange attraction to him. Yes, I will ride with him tomorrow morning and when I return, I will know."

Mary Sumner looked at Laura with love and compassion. Deep into Laura's eyes, she saw a smile of affection, but not the passionate excitement that prevailed when Laura spoke of her special friend. Mary hugged Laura gently and and smiled knowingly.

* *

At just a few minutes before eight o'clock the following morning, Jeffrey Marlowe arrived at the Sumner farm yard. He was riding his steel gray and leading a beautiful saddled bay mare. The mare was sleek and solidly built with dark mane and tail, four white stockings, and a blazed face.

Laura appeared at the steps of the porch. Her riding attire was a simple denim riding skirt with red checkered blouse, open at the collar.

Her hair was pulled back in a bun for the ride. Her apparel gave little doubt that she was an expert horsewoman.

"Jeffrey, she's beautiful."

"I told you that I would bring one of my best. Her name is Xavria. She has already borne a magnificent colt for me. Here, let me help you."

Jeffrey held the reins and left stirrup for Laura. Laura placed her left boot into the stirrup, grabbed the saddle horn and swung easily up into the saddle. Jeffrey handed her the reins, then walked around them to mount his gray.

They turned as one and rode slowly out of the yard toward the east, visiting casually as they left the farm.

* *

At mid-afternoon, Carroll and Mary Sumner had just returned from Sunday services at church and were getting out of the ranch wagon. They turned to notice a single rider approaching. He was leading a beautiful coal black stallion.

Both watched carefully as the man rode toward them and turned into their farm yard. He was tall, lanky, and rode easy in the saddle. He wore Levi's, a blue shirt, faded bandana, a dark colored jacket, and black Stetson.

Mary Sumner recalled the conversation with Laura and became immediately interested in this visitor.

The rider drew up slowly to the hitching post in the front yard. The couple looked him over. He appeared to be a man in his mid thirties. He had sandy hair, with smiling blue-green eyes and a warm smile.

"Howdy," he called out as he tipped his Stetson. "Is this the Sumner farm?"

"Hello to you. Yes. I am Carroll Sumner and this is my wife, Mary."

The stranger's face spread into a silly grin that resembled a little boy who had just sneaked a cookie from the pantry. "Then I am at the right place. I am Cole Stockton, a friend of Laura. I suppose she is with you?"

"Mr. Stockton, Laura went riding with an old friend early this morning. They should be back most anytime. Please, come in and have some coffee, and maybe a cinnamon roll or two."

"Ma'am, you just spoke the magic words. Let me tie up at your hitching rack."

The Sumners watched as Cole Stockton dismounted. The first thing that caught their eye was the gunbelt around his slim waist. He turned to face them and they saw more clearly the manner in which he wore his gun. It was low to wrist level, the way of an experienced gunfighter.

Stockton stepped forward and held out his hand to Carroll Sumner. They shook hands and Mr. Sumner found that the shake was firm and friendly, not cold and lifeless as he had seconds before imagined. Stockton's face was one of a man of honor.

Mary Sumner continued to study this stranger who professed to be a friend of her daughter. Their eyes met. She saw a gentleness that reflected honesty and integrity. The mother smiled warmly and held out her hand. She felt the warmth that radiated from this man.

"Please, come into the house. I'll put some coffee on. It will only take a little while. Are you from Colorado, Mr. Stockton?"

"Well, I seem to be now. I was born and raised west of here during the early days of the Republic. Traveled a great deal after I left home—still do."

* *

Jeffrey guided Laura as they rode. Before long, they were at the special place along the creek, where they stopped in times past. The place was still peaceful with a beauty of its own. Colorful wildflowers bloomed in abundance. Laura remembered the warm kisses that they shared then. This was the place, where they had promised to marry so long ago.

Jeffrey dismounted and held his arms up to Laura. She hesitated briefly, but smiled and let him help her down. They strolled to the creek bank and stood watching the flowing clear water. A cool breeze caught a wisp of Laura's hair. Once in a while, the gentle splash of a trout interrupted the stillness. Jeffrey gently turned Laura to face him.

"Dearest Laura. I am deeply sorry that I hurt you. I was a complete fool for even looking at another woman. Now, my days are empty. I think of you often. Yesterday when our eyes met, my heart brightened for the first time in years. I would like to start over again. Things will be different, I promise you."

Laura looked deep into Jeffrey's eyes. She saw both the remorse and the spark of hope. Laura lowered her eyes and was silent for a long moment. Finally, she spoke.

"Jeffrey. You were my first real love and for that, I will always hold a special place in my heart for you. It can never be the same. Our lives are different now. There is another, whom I met in the wilds of Colorado. Maude Pritchard predicted it, but I didn't understand it then. Now, I do. I have found my destiny. This man loves me for myself. He stands beside me during the best and the worst of times. He lets me be myself. He treats me with honor and respect, even during those times on the ranch when I have had little time for him. He has always been there for me. No, Jeffrey. My place is with him."

Jeffrey was without words. He studied Laura carefully before he spoke. "He is a very lucky man, Laura. I see it in your eyes. Your eyes shined with love even as you spoke of him. I'm sorry that I brought you here today. Please forgive me."

"Jeffrey. It's all right. It was good to return to our place of joy for this conversation. This was our place once. I'm glad we rode here today. It made me see things so very clearly. Thank you."

"Come, Laura. I will take you back home now. Thank you for being honest with me."

They mounted and turned their horses back toward the Sumner farm. An hour later, they rode into the yard and Laura's face lit up like a thousand stars on a clear night. Her eyes filled with tears of joy. They shined brightly and a big smile spread across her face. Jeffrey noticed the change in her immediately.

Laura heeled Xaveria to the hitching post, literally jumped out of the saddle, dashed around a dark chestnut horse to throw her arms around a small black one.

"Mickey! I've missed you so much. Did you miss me?"

Jeffrey was stunned when Laura hugged and kissed the horse. The black returned his feelings when he nuzzled her face and shoulder. Laura spoke softly and caringly to him. The black horse nuzzled her again as if he understood every word Laura said.

The door opened just then and Carroll and Mary Sumner stepped out to the porch. Close behind them was a tall, lanky man dressed in trail clothes. The most striking thing about him to Jeffrey was the manner in which he wore his gunbelt. Without a doubt, this man was intimate with that Colt.

Cole Stockton stepped off the porch and stood back a bit from Laura and Mickey. Suddenly, Laura looked up into those blue-green eyes and everyone—everyone, including Jeffrey—felt the heat of their bond. Laura smiled and then rushed into Cole's arms. The kiss was long and warm and genuine.

"Cole! I'm so glad to see you. Thank you for bringing Mickey with you. I've missed you both terribly."

After an awkward few moments for Jeffrey, Laura graciously introduced him to Cole. The men shook hands. Jeffrey now knew what brand of devotion he lost in those days past. He regretted that Laura could never be his. Yet, he felt a joy for her. She had truly found her destiny.

Mary Sumner placed her arm around her husband and held him tightly. Their embrace mirrored the younger couple. They knew that Laura was definitely in love, and they felt happy for her.

Jeffrey stayed only briefly, then turned to his horses. Laura followed him. Before he mounted, she kissed him lightly on the cheek.

"Goodbye, Jeffrey. I hope you find what you need."

"Goodbye, Laura. I wish you both every happiness."

Jeffrey rode slowly away towards his ranch, never looking back.

* *

Over a Sunday supper of roasted chicken, and all the trimmings, Mr. and Mrs. Sumner outlined the events that led to their current troubles.

Cole listened intently to their story. The situation was familiar fare to him. A ruthless rancher needed more range and water for his cattle. To obtain it, he would first investigate those neighboring small spreads to find any bank notes on them. The greedy rancher would use strong argument to the effect that the small farmer or rancher would not be able to pay the note due to droughts, poor management of his farm, dropping prices, or increased production costs. Finally, he would coerce the local banker into selling him the note at a small loss.

The selfish rancher knew all too well that the small farmer or rancher would not be able to pay the note due to droughts, poor management of his farm, dropping prices, or increased costs on their main product.

Once the bank sold the note to the corrupt rancher, the law allowed the holder of the note to demand payment in full within ninety days or vacate the premises. Many small farms were lost in this manner and large ranches became even larger. Most of these ranchers would hire known gunmen, vicious killers, to enforce their demands.

Usually, the settlers had no recourse. Having no money to pay, they would up and leave, allowing the rancher to move in. Those farmers or small ranchers that resisted were subject to night raids, barns mysteriously burned, stock slaughtered, fields burned out, and their families harassed. It also happened that some men would be goaded into a gunfight, and killed in front of their families.

Often, displaced widows with children could only find menial work in neighboring towns where the family sank into a life of poverty and squalor.

The local law usually made an attempt to bring justice. On occasion, the men of the law actually conspired against the small ranchers and farmers. There were even instances of the local lawmen being run off or killed, in order to accommodate the wishes of an evil rancher.

Sometimes, small farmers would band together, hiring their own gunmen. The arming of both sides brought an all out range war where both sides suffered deadly consequences.

Cole Stockton listened to their story, and then Laura apprised him of the breed of gunman employed by Charles Farnum. She also told him of her exchange of words with Chase Logan.

Cole reflected on the name. "I know Chase Logan. Wherever he surfaces, his favorite henchmen are sure to be close behind. He may have joined forces with two men by the name of Jake Pender and Bob Strahan. All three are vicious in a gunfight and will provoke a lesser man to draw against one of them; then all three will shoot him at the same time to insure their planned outcome."

Cole paused for a moment or so before continuing, "Mr. Sumner, I highly suspect that one or all three of these men will come here looking for you. I agree with Mary and Laura. Do not wear your gun. Laura is right. Let her wear the gun. She's very good with it and knows how to handle whatever may come up. I could be here also, if I may stay here at your house. I'll deal with the situation, and they ain't going to like it one bit. I do believe that they may start early tomorrow morning. We'll be ready for them."

* *

As Cole sat on the front porch rolling himself a smoke later that evening, he quietly surveyed the layout of the Sumner farm. He methodically memorized every place that could be used as cover by raiders.

Laura retired to her old room to prepare for bed. A light rap came at the door. It was her mother. "Laura, dear, I see now why you were reluctant to answer many questions about Mr. Stockton. He is a professional gunfighter, isn't he?"

"Yes, Mother, he is. He is a very good one. He is well known in parts north and west of here. He was even a friend to Wild Bill Hickock."

"Well, dear, we visited a bit before you and Jeffrey returned. I believe that he must be a good man also. I am certain that your father holds him in high regard also. I understand now, why you haven't married. I tend to shudder when I think of the times that he must face vicious men and wonder how you would cope. Maybe he could just give up his guns and get a ranch or farm."

"Mother, I kept it from you, until you and Father could meet him. He has a job. Cole Stockton is a United States Marshal. He seldom wears his badge when traveling, but when the time comes, you will see him pin on the silver star."

"He is a federal marshal? We had no idea. Laura, your father and I believed him to be a hired gun. We are proud to have him stay with us. Goodnight dear, I must tell your father."

"Don't worry. Cole will handle everything. You must put your trust in him. Good night, Mother."

Chapter Thirteen

Trouble Around Every Corner

As the sun rose over the land, a half dozen somber hired gunmen rode together slowly. They moved through fields recently plowed on the Sumner farm, lined up abreast. The men stopped in that same line in front of the Sumner house. Their leader, Chase Logan, called out in a harsh voice, "Sumner! Carroll Sumner! Come out here to face us!"

Each gunman believed that because it was early, the family would find themselves unprepared for their visit. Their intent was to alarm Mr. Sumner, causing him to grab his gun before he stepped out to the porch. According to their plan, when he showed himself with gun in hand, they would fill him with lead, only to leave the man's body lying where he fell.

The front door opened slowly. Laura Sumner appeared and stepped out on the porch, in her everyday work clothes. The Colt Lightning was strapped around her slim waist. She held a determined look on her face as she faced Chase Logan.

"What do you want, Mr. Logan? You are not welcome here."

"Well, now! The *Lady* is packing iron like she knows how to use it. What is your intent, Missy? You aim to shoot all six of us? Why there ain't no way in hell a woman can take the likes of us."

A steady voice rose from nowhere interrupted the conversation. "Maybe not Logan, but, I can and will, starting with you."

Logan froze in the saddle, his hands held stationary. The voice originated behind them, the voice of cold, lethal action should anyone even look like they would touch a gun.

"Sit easy, men," commanded Logan. "They've snuck someone up behind us."

The stern voice came again, "I was in the barn when I saw you fellers coming through the field. That is not the proper way to enter this farm. You should have used the road."

Cole Stockton walked cautiously around the group to position himself on to the porch and stand with Laura. His eyes met Logan's eyes and held steady.

Logan felt the icy chill of his soul burning in hell as Stockton's piercing glance penetrated his thoughts. Logan quickly averted his gaze for a moment, only to look back to find that Stockton never flinched. A shiver shook through Logan's body. He had never in his life felt so vulnerable. Sweat beads formed across his forehead while his palms became slick.

"Just who are you, Mister and what is your stake in this?"

"Well, Logan. I heard that you wanted to meet the *lily livered gent* that would be a friend to this lady. Here I am. Now, what are you going to do about it? Would you like to say it again—to my face?"

Chase Logan suddenly saw his life flash before his eyes. He felt his soul burning in the hell fires of this man's eyes. He shook his head to the negative and dropped his head.

"I thought so. Alright, Logan, I'm going to give you some advice. First, before you tend to make a brash statement, find out who or what the friend is. Next, you take your men there and you ride back to Charles Farnum. You tell him that if there is any trouble, Cole Stockton will come for him and he ain't going to like it one bit."

Cole Stockton! The name reverberated through Logan's mind like a bolt of thunder. He had heard of Cole Stockton and the word was *lethal*. Stockton was considered one that you surely did not want to cross.

"I'll tell him. Like you said, he ain't going to like it."

"You just tell him, Logan. One other thing. If you or your friends are with him when trouble starts, I'll hunt you down and shoot you where I find you. Do I make myself clear?"

"Yah, I understand," related Logan. "One day it will be just you and me and its coming fast." Logan intended to get in one more threat before Stockton threw them off the Sumner farm.

"Ride out, Logan, before I change my mind."

The six riders turned their mounts slowly to carefully ride out. Each man deliberately kept his hand away from his gun. They knew who Cole Stockton was and if Chase Logan wouldn't draw against him, no one would. They walked their horses to the gate before they broke into a fast trot down the road.

Logan breathed easier as he put distance between himself and the Sumner farm. He cursed silently under his breath, "Damn! I don't like not knowing what I'm up against. I should've asked the name of her friend. Cole Stockton is in town and now this job ain't what it was cracked up to be. I gotta figure this one out. We are going to have to take on Stockton if we are to finish this job. I've known men who tried and they are stone cold dead and buried."

* *

Laura turned to face Cole. She felt confused by his behavior toward Logan and his men. "You just let them go, Cole! You know they were here to kill my father. Now they will be lying for you somewhere as well."

"I suspect that they will, Laura. I had to let them go. They haven't really done anything yet, except trample down some of your father's newly plowed field. By the way, I have some help coming. I have three ex-Texas Rangers who will be staying at the St. Charles Hotel in town."

Cole continued, "They will be making inquires about this land scheme and also using influence to gather information from other locations where these men have caused trouble. Once we piece it all together, the four of us will pay them guys a visit they won't quickly forget."

Laura retorted, "Correction, Cole! Five of us will pay them a visit. I'm mad as hell and I want in on this. No one plans to kill my father and just gets away with it."

"Hell hath no fury." Cole coughed into the back of his hand.

"What?" Laura demanded.

"Just repeating a saying I heard once. By the way, you never mentioned whether you had the money to pay off that note or not. Do you?"

"No, Cole. You know I don't have that kind of money. I do have about five hundred that I can put toward it though. That leaves fifteen hundred for my parents to raise in less than two months. I have worried and wondered where to get the remainder. My folks sure don't have it."

"Why don't you consider this. Wire the bank in Denver. Ask Homer Olsen if he would invest two thousand against this homestead. Agree to throw in some of your Colorado land holdings from the ranch as collateral, if that seems necessary. Let him ponder it for a day or so. I will wire Judge Wilkerson. Olsen owes him a favor. We'll just see what transpires. I would like nothing better than to ride up to Charles Farnum and hand him the entire note, just to see his face."

"I want to do that myself, Cole."

Cole responded with a concerned voice, "O.K., but it could be dangerous. No telling what Farnum will do. He will be angry at best and want revenge. That's exactly how I want Charles Farnum—frustrated."

Cole followed with, "Laura. You should stay here at the farm. I am going into town and see if my friends have arrived yet. I should be back by supper time."

Laura laughingly broke the tension, "There you go, Cole, thinking about your stomach again."

"Well, Laura. Your mother has spoiled me with them great vittles. No wonder you cook so well. You had a good teacher."

Laura blushed a bit, but beamed radiantly with the pride that only a daughter could have for the culinary talents of her mother. She smiled at Cole as she leaned forward to kiss him lightly on the cheek.

"That's for your kind words, Sir," she whispered into his ear. "I'll pass them on to Mother."

Cole headed over to the barn with a grin on his face. He saddled up Warrior. He led out of the barn, put boot to stirrup and swung easily into the saddle. He lightly touched Warrior's flanks with his spurs. The stallion broke into an easy lope down the road towards town.

Stockton had gone no more than a few miles when the distant crack of a rifle caught his attention. He pulled up short to listen. Another shot. He rode at a gallop toward the sound of gunfire.

The terrain around Dallas was mostly rolling hills. Tall grasses and thick stands of mesquite gave way periodically to heavy brush.

"Well, Warrior. The shots came from just about here. Let's look careful now."

Warrior responded as if he understood every word. Cole rode cautiously through heavy mesquite, Colt Revolver at the ready. Then, in a small clearing, he caught slight movement.

The marshal dismounted and approached quietly, ever so slowly on foot. Warrior trailed close behind. A magnificent steel gray stallion stood nuzzling a form on the ground.

Stockton moved carefully forward. He listened carefully. There was only silence. Cole neared the prone form to find Jeffrey Marlowe lying face down in the grass. He had been shot in the back, twice.

Cole carefully searched the surrounding area with a sweep of his eyes. Nothing moved. No sound came. He thought, "Whoever did this believed that two bullets were enough. They never checked the body, or I interrupted. They didn't want to be seen, so they lit out."

The experienced marshal knelt at Jeffrey's side and turned him over carefully. He leaned down close to Jeffrey's face. The man was still breathing. He was seriously wounded, but alive.

Cole tore open Jeffrey's fine linen shirt to examine his wounds. One bullet had passed through his right shoulder. The second shot had hit his lower back some three inches from his spine. Cole assumed that the second bullet was still in there.

Cole got up, went to his saddlebags and produced a spare shirt. He withdrew his pocketknife and cut the garment into strips and patches. He folded a patch over each wound, and bound them tightly to stop the bleeding. Next, the lawman reached down and pulled Jeffrey up to a standing position. Cole half carried, half dragged him toward the gray. The gray shied away. Cole called to Warrior. "Warrior! Come help me pin this horse in."

Warrior trotted to the opposite side of the gray and nudged it closer to his master. The gray stallion seemed to understand and stood stationary.

Cole steadied the wounded man against the steel gray. He lifted him up and over, to place the limp body across the saddle. He reached over and taking the lariat, secured the fallen man across the saddle.

"Got to get him to a safe place. Back to the Sumner's farm, that's the closest. I wonder why they bushwacked him. He is too prominent to be involved in this land scheme, unless the man found out something worth killing him over."

After mounting Warrior, Cole took up the gray's reins and led out back toward the Sumner farm.

* *

Laura and her parents sat on the front porch of the farmhouse enjoying a cool glass of lemonade along with freshly baked cookies when a rider and led horse came down the road. Laura watched the rider for a few seconds before she was sure who it was.

"That's Cole! There must be something wrong. He's leading a gray horse. My God! That's Jeffrey's horse and that must be Jeffrey lying over the saddle. What has happened?"

Cole eased back on the reins and slowed to a stop, letting the gray ease up along side of him at the hitching rack. He swung down.

"Laura. Set a fire to get some hot water going. Mr. Sumner, help me with this man. He has been shot, but is alive. There's a bullet that needs to come out."

Mary Sumner turned to Laura. "I'll move everything off of the kitchen table and put in the leaves. I'll spread my old tablecloth over it. It is clean. You get the fire going and water to boiling. Then, get your father's bag from the attic."

Laura nodded as she ran into the house. She felt too frightened to speak. Mary Sumner was close behind. Carroll Sumner and Cole Stockton discussed how they would carry the body of a limp Jeffrey Marlowe into the house. Once there, they would lay him gently on the kitchen table.

Stockton lifted Marlowe off his horse and the two men carried the unconscious wounded man into the house. The covered table was ready for the patient.

Cole ripped the shirt off Jeffrey. He bent closer and listened to the man's shallow breathing. "We got to do this fast. I want him to live so he can tell me what he knows about this shooting."

Laura Sumner appeared in the kitchen doorway. She silently held a small black bag out to her father. Mary Sumner turned to her husband. "You can do it, dear. Just think about it and it will come back to you."

Carroll Sumner swallowed hard. He hadn't seen that black bag since the Civil War. He hadn't touched those instruments in more than ten years. The older gentleman had been a surgeon's assistant during the war where he had learned firsthand the techniques of removing rifle shot and bullets from numerous parts of a human body. He had seen the worst of wounds. During occasions when a surgeon was not available, he was even expected to perform emergency surgery to save a life.

Mr. Sumner didn't say a word. Cole immediately grasped the nature of his hesitation.

"Doctor Sumner. You are the most qualified. You have it to do."

"But, I'm not a doctor. I was only a surgeon's assistant on the battlefield."

"Mr. Sumner—Carroll. You are the closest thing to a doctor this man has. You're his only chance to live. You must do it."

"Suppose I slip. Suppose I make a mistake?"

"He won't know the difference, neither will anyone else in this room."

"But, I will."

Cole countered, "I trust in you. You know that your wife and daughter trust in you." During this conversation Laura had opened the dusty bag to find the instruments. She had already placed them in a line on the table.

After carefully washing his hands and forearms with hot water and soap, Carroll Sumner moved close to Jeffrey. He wiped his forehead. He closed his eyes in prayer, and then took a deep breath. Mary stood as his assistant, herself in silent prayer. He exhaled. He swallowed hard, then carefully pulled back the makeshift bandage on the imbedded bullet wound.

He took his finger and slipped his index finger into the wound, probing for the feel of lead. He located it two inches into Jeffrey's lower back. He felt around slowly, but methodically.

"He's very lucky. The bullet didn't break up, but it is close to the spine. I think I can get it."

Sumner called to Laura for the instruments he would need. He asked for a clean linen napkin to place near Jeffrey's back. Several minutes ticked by. Mary Sumner picked them up and, one by one slipped them into boiling water. A few minutes ticked by. Mary took a pair of tongs and one by one, lifted the sterilized instruments from the pot to lay them neatly in line on the clean linen table napkin.

The wife stood near her husband and a whisper came from her lips, "Do it, Carroll. I know you can do it."

Mr. Sumner swallowed hard once again. He looked carefully at the instruments and selected the probe and a scalpel. He moved to Jeffrey's side. He began the arduous task of sliding the instrument into the wound to grasp the bullet. Sweat trickled down his brow as his wife stepped forward with a towel to wipe it away.

Cole Stockton observed Laura. He read her thoughts. He moved near her to gently touch her arm. He reached to brush a solitary tear from her cheek, then took her hand in his and led her out to the porch. Cole took her into his arms and held her tightly for a long moment. Her body shivered against him.

Laura raised her face to question Cole. "Why was he shot? He's not part of this."

"Laura, I figure that he knows something, or learned something that he wasn't supposed to. Considering where I found him, he just might have been on his way here to your parent's farm. I'm going to ride back there to look around, then, I'm going to pay a visit to the local law. Keep Jeffrey here and don't say a word to anyone about this."

"I understand. Cole, Jeffrey was my first love. We had planned to marry, but the bond was broken. It was before I met you. I wanted you to know that."

"Cole, you know by now that there is no one but you. Yes, of course, I wish Jeffrey no harm."

"I know, Laura. I know. I've got work to do. Watch him closely and when he comes around, ask him what he knows."

"I will do that, Cole."

Laura moved closer to Cole, wrapped her arms around him and kissed him with an intensity that could have ignited a forest fire. Their bond of love was more sound than ever.

* *

It took a painstaking hour, but Carroll Sumner extracted the bullet from Jeffrey Marlowe's lower back. He poured a generous amount of anesthetic liniment over the wound to disinfect it. Next, he took the poker from the fireplace and thrust it deeply into the hot coals of the wood stove, watching it slowly turn red hot. He pulled it out, blew on it to remove the ash and then, drew it along the bullet hole. The hot iron cauterized the wound.

Carroll Sumner placed the poker back at the fireplace. He turned to his wife and daughter with solemn face and sweaty brow. The farmer sighed.

"I've done everything I know. Only time will tell now." Mary Sumner was the first to hug him closely. Next, Laura whispered into his ear, "Thank you, Father. I know that you did your best. Jeffrey will be most grateful."

Chapter Fourteen

Help Arrives

Originally named the Dallas Hotel, the St. Charles was founded by Sarah Horton Cockrell, about the year 1860 after the previous St. Nickolas Hotel burned down in a major fire that destroyed much of downtown Dallas.

The St. Charles became a favorite place of rest and board for cattlemen and travelers going West. The bar with card tables afforded a place for the conversation of gentlemen. Justin Cooper, Josh Slater, and Jim Farley arrived in Dallas and checked in to the St. Charles Hotel. Following a check in, the trio each dropped his gear in his room. They decided to hang around the lobby and observe other guests.

The plan was that Cole Stockton would be there in early afternoon to fill them in on the reason for their summons.

Cooper rustled up a copy of *The Dallas Daily Herald*, and began to read up on the local news. Josh thumbed through a recent copy of *Harper's magazine*. He enjoyed national news of politics, literature and the arts. His prime interest, though, was the reviews of new novels recently published. The artwork was also a favorite of his.

Jim Farley took a rocker on the front porch of the hotel and with his pocketknife in hand busied himself by whittling on a stick he found in the street. His intent was people watching as well as getting the lay of the land.

* *

Cole Stockton rode back to the ambush site. He dismounted to look carefully around the spot where he'd found Marlowe. In an hour's time, he found the tracks of the assailant, two empty rifle cartridges, and the remnants of tobacco spit.

Cole analyzed in true investigative fashion. He thought, "This man chews a lot. Favors a Winchester 44.40, probably carries a .44 on his belt. By the tracks, he didn't wait for Marlowe, he followed and overtook him. Probably hit Marlowe in the shoulder first and when he didn't fall out of the saddle, shot him the second time. He shot fast and probably jerked the round, which caused him to miss his main target area and hit the lower back instead of high middle. Looks like his horse might have shied back a bit at the first gunshot. It could have been a borrowed horse. A trusted horse would not have moved like that. These tracks show a worn shoe on the right front. The shooter turned suddenly to gallop away. That was probably when he heard me. He surely did not want to be recognized. I'll follow these tracks a while and see where they lead."

Stockton swung into the saddle and carefully followed the tracks left by the bushwhacker. They led directly to the Diamond "F," the Farnum Ranch.

"I thought as much," mumbled Cole. "One more fact to add to this situation. Well, there are probably too many to take on myself. I'll just hold this information for the right time, and then, Charles Farnum and I will have it out."

Cole turned Warrior toward town. He would speak with Justin Cooper and his Ranger friends.

* *

In the meantime, Charles Farnum was violent in his anger. He ranted and cursed about how, "Any man worth his salt would have drawn his gun and shot that damn Stockton dead right there. I would've! Damn his soul."

Farnum continued, "Figure that! A lady hooked up with a gunfighter. I never would have imagined that. Well, we'll see about it. There are two herds of cattle coming from raids in the next couple of days. One from below the border, and one from New Mexico. Once I have all of my riders together, we will run over that Sumner land. I expect to trample down every blade of grass, every plant, and everything in our wake. I'll accept nothing less than complete destruction of the Sumner farm. We'll kill anyone who stands in our way and burn everything in sight. I need that land for the water. Without the Sumner farm, I can't water all those cattle coming to me."

Farnum scowled at Chase Logan. "Logan—you thought yourself good with the gun. That's why I hired you and your boys. I'll pay you two thousand dollars extra each to kill Cole Stockton. I don't care how you do it. Just do it. And, do it soon."

With those final words, Farnum turned on his heels and moved into his study. He slammed the door after himself, uttering a stream of heated profanity heard by all in the outer room.

Logan, Strahan, and Pender stood there looking at each other. The boss had just issued an order. They would make money, should they succeed. Each knew that many before them had tried and they were cold in the ground.

Two thoughts came to mind. Charles Farnum had lost all sense of reality, and secondly, that no one man alive was going to take Cole Stockton in a stand up gunfight. That was suicide. It meant that the three of them together must face one of the most deadly gunfighters in the West. A question immediately formed in each man's mind.

"Who will live and who will die? Who wanted to be the first to face this man, Stockton? Who wanted to be directly in front of him when his hand fluidly slipped to his holster and with lightning speed drew, cocked, and fired that deadly Colt Revolver?"

The answer was simple—none of these three men wanted to be that first target.

Each man recalled stories about Cole Stockton drawing to shoot four or five men in succession. Word had it that Stockton would stand ready to take lead and calmly reload. Times were told of a wounded Stockton continuing to stand and fire that Colt. He would take careful aim and shoot his adversaries stone cold dead.

As those thoughts came, each man felt fear grip his mind. No man dared look at the other two.

* *

Jim Farley was the first to see Cole riding toward the hotel. He eased out of the rocker, set the whittling aside, and folded his pocketknife. He stepped to the door of the hotel to wait while Cole tied Warrior at the hitching rack and water trough. Cole glanced up to spot Farley and grinned. The men shook hands and then moved inside to the lobby to meet with Cooper and Slater.

"Look what I found out in the street," announced Jim as they neared their two friends. They all shook hands and Cole offered, "Let's get a cool beer."

They moved through the batwing doors to the hotel bar, got a mug of beer each and then gathered at a table in the back of the room. The three Ranger friends leaned toward Cole as he spoke in a low voice.

"First off, I thank each of you for coming. I knew that I could count on you. Now, Laura Sumner's parents are in danger of losing their farm to an unscrupulous rancher named Charles Farnum. The Texas drought here has devastated farms and ranches. They must have water to survive. Farnum has bought up their mortgage as well as some other land with a creek or water access in order to expand his cattle empire. He has a number of rowdies to back him up. He also has hardened gunmen, namely Chase Logan, and his henchmen in on the deal." The ex-Rangers exchanged knowing looks.

Cole sipped his beer before continuing, "The Sumners have about sixty more days to come up with the money to pay off the note. Arrangements are in process to provide that money. Personally, I don't think that Farnum is going to wait that long. He can't afford to lose the Sumner farm by them paying it off. He's already sent Logan and his boys to face off with Mr. Sumner and goad him into a fight. I put a damper on that for the time being."

Cooper interjected, "And you think that Farnum and all his boys are going to try something drastic, like a raid on the Sumner farm?"

Cole nodded, "I think that it's coming very soon. In fact, one of Farnum's men shot and wounded a neighbor horse rancher named Jeffrey Marlowe today and left him for dead. I came upon Marlowe and took him to the Sumner place. Mr. Sumner is patching him up. We are waiting for him to come around to ask him questions and hopeful that he can provide some answers. I think he saw or found out something about Farnum and they decided to eliminate him. Anyway, that's the current situation. What do you think, boys?"

Josh Slater stroked his chin whiskers a spell before speaking, "Cole, I'm wondering just where this Farnum guy is getting all this cattle to build his empire with. Suppose, just suppose now, that he is stealing cows from afar and running them up here."

Jim Farley offered his thoughts, "Either way, if he has got a goodly number of hard men with him, then, he will need a real good reception when he and his boys show up. Count me in on that reception committee, Cole."

Justin Cooper nodded his agreement and offered, "I know the Ranger Captain here in Dallas. I will pay him a visit this afternoon to hear what he might know." He turned to his two partners, "Let's get to work and see what we can find out. Cole, let's meet in my room here at the hotel tomorrow afternoon. We might just have some new information to our advantage."

The four men shook hands as Stockton left to go back to the Sumner farm. The Ranger friends decided that the best way to serve the situation was to split up to investigate the rancher's activities.

Jim Farley spent most of his time doing what he did best. That would be sitting in a chair along the boardwalk of the saloon nearest the Sheriff's Office. In this manner, he observed the saloon crowd, the local law force, and picked up a great deal of gossip from passing cowboys.

Cooper went to visit with Captain Will Hodges, Texas Rangers. After an hour with his old friend of Ranger years, Coop roamed down to the stockyards, talked cows with those who would pass the time, and befriended several young drovers.

Josh Slater did what he did best. He merely sat at a back table in a saloon known as a rustler hangout, and listened.

During the rest of that day and into the next, they passed one another on the streets of Dallas several times, yet never acknowledged each other. They were working.

* *

That same afternoon in Denver, Colorado, Homer Olsen, as a trustee and head banker at the Bank of Colorado, read the telegram for the second time. Homer had become a man of many acquaintances with whom he had done business throughout the years. Judge Wilkerson was one of those men.

Homer now pondered the request from Laura Sumner. "Laura is asking this bank for two thousand dollars against her parents' farm in Dallas. That land should be worth three times that amount in the water rights alone. Besides, that is Laura asking. She works honestly enough and her holdings are more than sufficient to cover that amount. I'll wire the money to the Dallas Bank this very afternoon."

The door to his private office suddenly opened and Judge Wilkerson determinedly walked into the room, closing the door behind him.

"Homer, I'm here because I got a telegram from Cole Stockton. He's down in Dallas and there's big trouble there—a land war, if you will."

Wilkerson paused for a moment to let his statement sink in to Homer's thoughts before continuing, "Laura Sumner needs two thousand dollars to help her family keep their farm. I want you to wire the entire amount and mark it for Cole Stockton only. There is going to be some heavy gunplay and we want to insure that the entire note is paid off without any consequences to the Sumner family."

"What? They are going to pay back the note, aren't they?"

"No, Homer. They will not pay back the note. The note will be paid from another source."

"Once again, Judge. You are not making any sense. I am loaning two thousand dollars to Laura Sumner's family, but neither she nor they will repay. I'm to give the money to U.S. Marshal Cole Stockton and there is some other entity that is going to repay this loan?"

"Yes, Homer. That's correct. There are hard men associated with the situation in Dallas, and some of them are wanted, with rewards posted. The amount of these rewards is more than sufficient to repay your loan."

"Joshua Wilkerson, you have absolutely dumbfounded me. Never in all my banking years have I had the sorry luck to stumble across a conniving pair of weasels such as you and Cole Stockton. You actually think that I, a respected banker, would stoop so low in spite of my investors, that I would let out a loan of such significant proportions that..."

"Oh, shut up with that wind bag stuff, Homer. Will you do it or not?"

"Did you bring one of your bottles of private whiskey with you?"

"Are you trying to intimidate or bribe a federal judge?"

"Hell, no! Are you trying to intimidate or bribe an officer of this bank, sir?"

"Hell no!"

"Well, then. Let's drink some of that wonderfully smooth whiskey before we go to see what Mildred Olsen, the local banker's wife has on the stove. Damn, it's good to see you, Joshua. Maybe we can play a couple of hands of poker tonight. Mildred loves to play. Besides, you can walk with me to the telegraph office to send a wire with the money. Then, dear friend, you owe me a rematch on that last chess game. You remember that game. It's the one where you got me drunk on your whiskey and then took advantage of me."

"Homer, if you weren't such a good friend and if my wife weren't your sister, I'd have locked up your sorry butt a long time ago, just for the shenanigans you've helped me pull over the past twenty years."

"Ah, Joshua, but it's been a very wonderful and interesting twenty years. Now, let's open that bottle of your private stock and enjoy ourselves with a man to man visit."

CHAPTER FIFTEEN

The Impending Storm

Near four o'clock the next afternoon the three Ranger friends sat quietly pondering their notes. A light rap came on the door of Justin Cooper's room. He moved to the door with Colt Revolver in hand. His companions drew their weapons, holding them at the ready. Coop opened the door just a crack, before he swung it open for Cole Stockton to join them.

"Howdy, boys, how's the rooms and the grub?"

Justin replied, "Well, Cole, we've had a damn sight better back at Penny's. Sit down. We've got a passel of news for you. First of all, there is a big land scheme going on. The local banker got scared with the big droughts of the last three years so he sold out the Sumner note to Charles Farnum. Farnum bought out the notes for six other small farms as well. As you might guess, each of these farms borders on his range. Now, looking at a map of the Dallas area, these farms run from the western side all the way down to the southern tip of Farnum's range. Now, what do you notice at a first glance?"

"I don't see anything, Coop. All I see is a man trying to expand his range."

"Exactly, Cole, but, if you were running stolen cattle from Mexico, or even New Mexico it is the shortest route into the stock yards and slaughter houses over at Fort Worth."

Cooper paused a moment to catch his breath, "Once there, the cattle are slaughtered, processed, packed and on the way to points East. No one would be the wiser. I believe that Farnum brings stolen herds onto his ranch from the southwest side where he holds them until he can get them to Fort Worth. He does this to circumvent the main trails. That is where the farm country lies."

Coop took a pencil and drew a line from Mexico directly into the southwest of Dallas. The line fell exactly across the farmland along the western side of Farnum's range. The Sumner farm held the most significant water source of this area.

Cole blurted, "Well, I'll be damned. That SOB is rustling cattle from Mexico and other places north of the border in his path. He has a smooth scheme running them across his range directly into the stockyards for immediate delivery. After a packinghouse does its work, there's no trace of his foul deeds. Taking those lands increases his holdings by one third, and in doing so, he has a clear route to disposing of the contraband for profit."

Coop continued with what he and his friends had learned. "You got it, Cole. Now, there is a lot more. It seems that half of Farnum's men are known gunmen. At least ten of them are wanted by the Rangers under different names. Hell, there is even a warrant, a long lost warrant, but still a warrant nonetheless, listed in Arkansas. It seems that Farnum's actual name is Stokely—Abner Stokely to be exact. Cole, the warrant is for murder. It seems that this Stokely character found his young bride on intimate terms with his partner. He killed them both in bed. Then, when tracked down and challenged by the local sheriff, the feller drew and killed him. Some identify Stokely as one of the first men that practiced the fast draw. He is presumably faster than scent off a skunk. That is pretty damn fast, I'd say."

"Yah, I can imagine. Now, there's Jeffrey Marlowe. Where does he come in?"

The old Ranger was eager to continue, "I'm glad that you asked that Cole. Let's take another look at that map. Look here. Marlowe's section ranges in a north-south direction. It lies precisely along the trail that any stolen stock from Mexico would take. I am going to say off hand, Cole, that Marlowe ran across a herd of strange cattle and wandered down for a better look. Perhaps someone saw him and decided that he was too dangerous to leave alive."

"That makes sense, Coop. My assumption is that someone followed and caught up with him, shooting him on the spot. I guess that I interrupted the attack when I came boiling up. I tracked those prints straight to the Diamond F Ranch—Farnum's spread."

Cooper had more to tell the marshal. "O.K., Cole. Josh found out some interesting things. Several of Farnum's riders patronized the saloon where Josh spent the afternoon while the rest of us were working."

Slater retorted with a grin, "I resent that, Coop. I was working, too. Well, I did have a real cool beer in my hand—mainly for show, of course."

"See what I mean, Cole. Some fellers just know what the good jobs are and take advantage of their partners. Anyway, shoot, tell him, Josh."

Josh Slater continued to tell the story. "Well, Cole, I overheard that there is going to be a big raid on a farm tomorrow morning. I believe it is the Sumner farm. It sounds as though there may be about fifty riders in that bunch. Their orders are to kill, trample, and burn everything in sight. Hell, one of them drunken hands even invited me to join them. He said that it would be their biggest day since stealing a Mexican Army herd last month. The feller bragged about a stolen herd on its way from New Mexico right now. I suspect it might be some of John Chisum's cows. From what I heard, it should be near the apex of the Farnum range just about sun up tomorrow."

The conversation was interrupted by a light rap at the door. Each man drew his weapon and cocked it. Coop went to the door as before and opened it a crack. He turned suddenly to his friends and opened the door wide. A lone man stepped into the room.

Cooper turned to Stockton, "Cole, let me introduce you to Captain Will Hodges, Texas Ranger. Will, this is Cole Stockton, United States Marshal."

"Marshal Stockton! This is a distinct pleasure. I know of your exploits and hold you in high esteem. I wish that you could have been one of us Texas Rangers, but we will do your bidding, as long as we get our men."

"Thank you, Captain. I have a deep respect for the Texas Rangers. I'm glad to have you and your men with us. Coop will fill you in on the particulars. I want to take those men who are running stolen cattle and who have plans to raid the Sumner farm. I want it understood that Charles Farnum, Chase Logan, Bob Stahan, and Jake Pender are mine and mine alone. You Rangers can claim all the rest. That is, all the rest standing after the smoke clears."

Cole continued. "Captain, I want Coop, Josh, and Jim Slater with me at the Sumner farm. You and your company of Rangers will ride in behind Farnum and his group to wait until we are attacked. Then, come with all haste. Send five of your Rangers to capture that herd. If you run them up the valley right into the Sumner farm, we can use them as a cavalry charge and break up the estimated fifty riders. From that point we're going to shoot hell out of those standing and the devil take the hindmost."

* *

The Sumner family moved Jeffrey Marlowe into Laura's room. They alternated watching him. Laura was with Jeffrey when his restlessness brought a moan. Laura moved quickly to his side. She dipped a clean washcloth into the basin on the night stand and gently wiped his brow. She spoke in a whisper,

"Jeffrey, don't move. Just lie still. You've been shot."

"But, Laura, how did I get here? I was on the way here to tell you and your friend something. Something hit me in the back. It felt as though fire burned inside of me."

"You must rest, Jeffrey. Cole found you and brought you to the farm. He and my father saved your life, Jeffrey. The man who shot you must've seen Cole coming and rode away before he could finish the job. Father removed the bullet. You must rest, now. Everything will be all right."

"No, Laura. I—I saw something." Jeffrey's voice trailed off, then his eyes opened wide and he continued, "I saw a large herd of strange cattle moving up the range between my ranch and your farm. I recognized some of Charles Farnum's men. I figure those cattle were stolen and that he is using our land, yours, and mine, to sneak them onto his ranch. Someone must have seen me and followed my trail."

Laura picked up the conversation, "That would make sense, Jeffrey. I'll tell Cole. Now, you must rest. Cole will take care of everything. I did not tell you before, Jeffrey, but Cole is a United States Marshal. He is working this situation. He should be back shortly. It is getting on to supper time, and Cole has never missed a good home cooked meal, if he could help it."

Jeffrey dozed which pleased Laura. He was exhausted. He exhaled, and his eye lids quivered before he fell into a deep asleep. Momentarily, Laura heard several voices from the kitchen. She quietly left the bedroom to see who had come to the farm.

Stockton stood in the center of the kitchen introducing Justin Cooper, Josh Slater, and Jim Farley to her parents. When Laura came in, he grinned that great big silly grin of his and held out his hand to her.

She was immediately at his side to meet Cole's Texas Ranger friends. There was an instant mutual admiration.

Cole spoke, "Mr. Sumner. We believe that your farm is going to become a battleground in the morning. You said that you wanted to fight for this farm. Well, this is your chance. We will need everyone who can handle a gun. I understand that there could be as many as fifty Farnum riders coming for you and we want to surprise them with a real warm welcome."

Mary Sumner interjected excitedly, "I can shoot. Not very well, but I can shoot. Somebody give me a gun."

Carroll spoke up, "Mary, you can use my Colt Navy, it should be light enough for you. I've got my Springfield rifle and double barreled shotgun. I'll be ready."

Laura related, "And I've got my Colt Lighting as well as the Winchester that you brought with Mickey."

Cole continued, "Each of these boys and I have two Colt revolvers and a rifle. Yes, I think that we will give Farnum and his boys a very warm welcome. Coop, where do you boys want to be?"

"Cole. I think that Josh and I will hold the barn. Jim can cover the back of the house. That leaves the four of you to take the full frontal attack. We'll catch them in a cross fire from the barn."

Cole thought for only a second, "One other thing, Coop. The last time Farnum riders were here, I stepped out from the barn. They just might have someone come in from your rear and check out the barn. They would want it for themselves."

"That's all right, Cole. We'll give them a good ole Ranger howdy."

Then, a second thought came to Cole, "By the way, Mr. Sumner. I stopped at the telegraph office on the way back here. I have a draft from the Bank of Colorado for two thousand dollars. We'll see that your note is paid in full to Charles Farnum. Does anybody have anything else to say? Now, is that a beef stew I smell simmering on the stove?"

Mary Sumner laughed. "Yes, Mr. Stockton. That is supper you smell. Let's all eat."

Laura looked deeply into Cole Stockton's eyes and she smiled that smile that spoke of a deep bond of love and admiration. He put his arm around her waist to give her a quick hug.

Josh Slater was the first to peer into the pot of stew. "My, but that stew does look good. Why Mrs. Sumner, we ain't had a decent meal since we left Fort Stockton over a week ago. Is that apple pie I smell? Apple pie is our most favorite of all. I can just taste that pie now."

"Don't worry, Mr. Slater. There is plenty to go around. Now, please everyone, give Laura and I a few minutes to set food out on the dining room table."

The lively bunch sat around the Sumner dining room table and enjoyed a hearty stew, fresh baked biscuits, butter, honey, and lots of good strong black coffee. There were two apple pies warm from the oven. The marshal and the Rangers put them away in no time.

CHAPTER SIXTEEN

Justice Quells the Storm

At four o'clock in the morning, Charles Farnum rose from his bed and began to dress. He donned his favorite Levi's, pulled on his most comfortable boots, strapped on a magnificent set of solid silver Mexican spurs, and then went to his hidden closet. He selected the shirt that he wore when he was *King of the Fast Draw.*

The shirt was black. He fashioned a silver colored puff tie around his neck before donning his vest. Next, he opened the locked drawer of his gun case. He withdrew a finely tooled, two-gun holster rig. He strapped it on, settling the gun belt into its most comfortable position. He admired himself in the full-length mirror.

Nodding affirmatively to himself, he then turned to his gun case. He looked, first, at the Navy .36 Colts that he had worn so proudly in his gun fighting days. He pondered them for several seconds.

Changing his mind, he reached into the case to withdraw two custom, ivory gripped, finely balanced Colt .44 Revolvers. He held them in his hands, balanced them for a split second, and then, twirled them around his fingers. He grinned devilishly as they spun perfectly into his holsters.

Charles Farnum then walked out of his ranch house and strode to the bunkhouse. He kicked the door open and rousted out his riders and hired gunmen. They viewed him with awe. They had never seen their boss dressed in this manner. He appeared even more menacing and evil.

Chase Logan swallowed hard. He knew Farnum was the sort of man who could turn a group of hardened men into a mob of destruction. "That fool is going to push those riders right onto the Sumner farm and there will be Hell to pay. Cole Stockton ain't no fool. This SOB thinks of himself as the gunfighter elite. He is going to get a lot of these men killed, for nothing."

Chase Logan slipped quietly out the door. He walked quickly to the stable and saddled his horse. He was leading out of the barn when Charles Farnum suddenly stood in his way.

"What? Is Chase Logan running out? Why, you sniveling coward, I am many times faster than Cole Stockton when it comes to dragging iron. I perfected the fast draw many years ago. I am Abner Stokley. Perhaps, you may have heard of me. I am a legend with my guns. There is no one faster nor more thorough in a gunfight."

Logan stared at Farnum. "Farnum, you are insane! You are living the past. You think that you can just walk in there to the Sumner farm and run over everyone and everything? You had better rethink your plans. Cole Stockton is waiting for you. Not only that, that woman wears iron like she was born with it. No, Farnum! I'll tell you straight out. You go into that Sumner farm and it will be the last thing that you ever do, because Cole Stockton will put so much lead into you that people will think that you are a cannon ball."

"So! My valiant knight has suddenly become a coward?"

"I hate to say it, Farnum, but I think that even I can beat your draw. You have put too many years on since your heyday."

"So be it, Logan. I never liked you from the beginning, and when you backed down from Stockton, I knew that you weren't the breed to pull this through for me. I am taking over. You have a choice, Logan. Make it now! Join us or pull that hogleg!"

Chase Logan stared at Farnum. He saw the fiery flames of hell. Logan gave him a quick somber smile. His thoughts spun to the eyes of a man that in one split second sent the fear of hell through his body— Charles Farnum was not that man. Logan knew that the only way out of this predicament was to draw his weapon.

Logan's hand swept to his Colt. His hand felt the familiar grip. He brought the revolver out of the holster. He was faster than ever before. His Colt had just cleared the holster when Charles Farnum's Colt thundered and the hot lead drove deep into Logan's chest.

Chase stumbled back against the wall of the stable. His eyes turned up and he passed into the world of the unknown. His limp hand released the cocked Colt Revolver.

Farnum looked down at the slain man and smiled. Yes, he still had the knack. He still had the skill. No one would stop him. Now, for the task at hand. His face was set. His riders would take the Sumner range.

He stood to gain a large sum of money from the sale of the stolen herds. He pursed his lips and nodded approval of what was about to happen.

Farnum stormed out of the stable and shouted to his waiting men, who were too afraid to question why he'd killed Chase Logan. Minutes later, a group of some fifty hardened gunmen and riders for the Diamond F rode out in the direction of the Sumner Ranch.

* *

When the Farnum group approached the Sumner range, the old man directed five of his men to ride ahead, with orders to position themselves in the Sumner barn. His mind raced, "From there, we'll throw a crossfire into that farm house that will sound like the Battle of Gettysburg. We'll control all of the farmyard, and Cole Stockton or not, we'll kill everyone, burn everything, and completely level all standing structures of this place. There'll be nothing left to even suggest that this property was a farm.

The five riders took off at a gallop. They circled around and arrived at the back of the Sumner barn a good fifteen minutes before the main body of Farnum's men approached from the front.

The five men were well suited to the task. They would take the barn, all livestock in it, and hold it while they fired round after round into the Sumner house. They each carried over two hundred rounds of ammunition. They were sure to get their task done.

Jim Alberts was the first to arrive at the rear of the Sumner barn. He found the back door barred, but the block and tackle to the loft was hanging neatly to his advantage. He rode confidently to the dangling ropes and began to shinny up. "Have that door open in a jiffy, fellers."

Alberts reached the top of the loft, took two steps, and looked straight into the grinning face of Josh Slater. "Howdy. You look lost. Welcome to the Sumner farm!"

The would-be raider slammed to the loft floor with a well placed Colt Revolver barrel laid on his skull. The others followed suit. Each one climbed up the rope, never thinking that someone should be opening the back door to the barn. Two Texas Rangers met them all. Before long, these five men lay heaped, gagged, and hog-tied in a corner of the barn loft.

From the loft, the two Rangers saw the magnitude of the attack. Farnum riders were deliberately riding their horses through the recently planted fields. The horse's hooves tore up the earth as they thundered toward the farmhouse.

* *

Jeffrey Marlowe wakened to the sound of a great many horses. As he glanced around the room, he recalled the conversation with Laura. Hurting, he wormed himself out of the bed and crawled to the door. He looked down the hall, then called out, "Laura! Laura! Come quickly, I want to help." Then, Jeffrey fell to the floor.

Laura Sumner moved to Jeffrey's side. She gently turned him onto his back and felt the man's forehead. "Jeffrey, you're hurt. You can't possibly be of any help to us right now. Let me help you into bed."

Marlowe took a deep breath and drew himself to a sitting position. "No, Laura! You must let me help fight these people." The aching of his wounds suddenly got the best of the man and he lay back on the bed pillows breathing hard. After a few moments, Jeffrey melted against the pillow into a deep sleep.

Laura Sumner smiled sweetly. "I told you to sleep, Jeffrey. That was a gallant gesture. But, it is not necessary in this situation."

Gunfire broke out at that moment. Laura quickly covered Jeffrey, and then rushed to the front of the house. Carroll Sumner already had begun firing his shotgun. Cole Stockton stood at the door, Winchester in hand. The muzzle was smoking as he turned to look at Laura.

"Laura, take my place here. I'm going to check on the rear of the house. Shoot everyone that rides past here. Shoot their horses if need be."

"Cole, you know that I won't do that," Laura frowned at the thought.

"Do what?"

"Shoot the horses."

"All right, have it your way. Do what you can."

Cole moved quickly toward the back of the house as Laura moved to the door. When she peered out, her eyes went wide. Mounted directly in front of the porch was Charles Farnum. His eyes were wild with vengeance as he screamed, "I'm here to kill the whole lot of you!"

Laura threw open the door and leveled her Winchester directly at Farnum. She squeezed the trigger. Her quarry's horse bolted quickly and the bullet whizzed through his shirtsleeve.

Farnum turned and yelled at her. "You! You're that *Lady from Colorado*. I'm going to kill you, too."

Laura looked straight at the fanatical gunman and cried out, the magic words, "Not if I get you first!"

Farnum sneered, "There is no one that can take me. My real name is Abner Stokely. I'm the most deadly gunman in the West!"

Laura levered the Winchester and found it empty. She tossed the rifle aside and glared at the evil man. Farnum regained control of his mount, and reined the roan to a sliding stop. He met her gaze. His eyes burned with hatred. His right hand Colt swept toward Laura as her own hand flashed to her belt.

The grips felt smooth as the revolver filled her hand. The Colt Lightning rose smoothly from her holster to line directly on Farnum's middle. She fired.

The horseman flung his body quickly to one side as he swore in a loud voice. The .38 caliber bullet whizzed past his middle. If he had been a split second slower, he would have been on the ground, shot through the stomach.

Farnum leveled his Colt at Laura Sumner and squeezed off. Smoke and fire belched from the bore of his Colt. He missed. Laura, too, had ducked behind the door casing. His bullet sailed into the far wall of the Sumner home. He was wild with rage now.

A random shot from a raider sailed into the porch pillar and splinters blossomed. Laura caught one sliver of wood in her right forearm. She flinched and fell back through the open door, dropping her Colt Lightning just inside.

Farnum forced his mount toward the front door and, facing Laura Sumner, lined his Colt up on her middle. He squeezed the trigger.

The loud crack of Cole Stockton's Colt split the din. Farnum bellowed with pain as the .44 caliber round smacked into his right side. The rancher's shot went wild as he jerked the trigger of his revolver. It slipped out of his hand, dropping to the ground. Farnum swore loudly and whirled his mount sharply to the left.

Stockton stepped out to the porch, a Colt revolver in each hand. He centered on Charles Farnum. The older man reined in his mount and dismounted on the far side of the animal. He covered the wound in his side with his right hand. The old gunman drew his left hand Colt, and then, shied his horse away.

"I'm going to end your life, Stockton!" he screamed.

Stockton's reply was to fire another round, this one sailing Farnum's hat high into the air. Farnum fired from the hip and Cole felt the breeze of that bullet whistle through his open vest flap and shirt to smack into the outer wall of the Sumner home. The two men faced each other with fire in their eyes and smoking Colt Revolvers in their hands.

Carroll Sumner, who was at the side window, dropped his shotgun and grabbed his precious daughter. He dragged her from the open door and then dived to the floor himself as at least ten rounds of heavy rifle fire slammed into the porch and framework of the house.

The entire Sumner farmyard was a scene of bright orange blossoms of fire, heavy gunsmoke, and flying lead. Several of the raiding gunmen already lay in grotesque heaps, attesting to the accuracy of the small band of defenders.

* *

Mary Sumner stood at a side window and carefully aimed and fired Carroll's Colt Navy Revolver. She was not an expert shooter, but she hit two of the rancher's men, wounding them. She held a determined look on her usually pleasant face as she lined up another shot. Without warning, a heavy bore rifle bullet zipped through her blouse and creased her right arm. Her injury flinched the shot with the pistol, but her bullet caught Luke McGavin straight in the middle as he dashed for cover.

Blood seeped along the sleeve of Mary Sumner's blouse. She looked down and swore, "Dammit, my blouse is ruined. Now I'm madder than a wet hen. Come and get it you, SOB's."

Both Carroll and Laura Sumner looked at Mary in disbelief. Neither could remember hearing Mary swear. Yet, neither felt disappointed in her salty language considering the situation.

Mary lined up and pulled the trigger once again. Her bullet grazed the rump of a horse. The animal reared, dumped its rider hard to the ground, and galloped off down the road. She grinned with immense satisfaction.

Carroll Sumner shook his head as he grabbed up his shotgun again and moved to the front window. A group of mounted raiders came galloping into sight firing their pistols at the house.

Carroll pointed the gun and pulled both triggers at once. He caught three Farnum riders with buckshot and they slipped off their horses to the ground.

Laura slammed the front door shut. She pulled the long splinter out of her forearm, then, rubbed it quickly to quell the sting. She didn't stop to bandage the wound just yet. She picked up her revolver from the floor and moved to the other window.

Two assaulting raiders dismounted and ran across the open space from the corral to the right side of the house. Laura swung her Colt to line up slightly ahead of them and squeezed off. The lead man pitched forward face down and didn't move. She cocked the hammer back and squeezed off at the second man. His right leg folded under him and he went down in a scream of pain.

Laura swept her side of the yard with the muzzle. More riders boiled into view and she emptied the cylinder at them in rapid succession. Three of the riders whirled their mounts and dismounted. They ran for whatever cover they could find.

* *

Justin Cooper and Josh Slater took toll with their Winchesters from the loft and front door of the barn. "Watch it, Coop! Two guys running to the right! Damn, I missed."

"I got them, Josh, here they come."

The two Farnum men reached safety at the corner of the barn. They then moved stealthily along the right side of the structure. Justin Cooper moved his Winchester barrel right along with them and when they were at the center of the right hand barn side, he squeezed off at the first man through the planks.

The front man jerked backward with the heavy 44.40 lead and the second man dived behind an old wagon before Coop could chamber another round.

"Josh, you ain't the only one that's slowing down. I should've had that guy, too. Cover the front. I'm going after him. We can't have one behind us."

Josh levered several rounds into the middle of mounted raiders, causing them to jump off their horses and run to cover. He chuckled to himself, "Yah, get down behind that water trough. I'll wet your whistle for you."

He fired two rounds through the planks of the wooden trough, and soaked them good. The two men sputtered as streams of water poured into their faces while trying to fire back at Josh Slater.

Coop moved to a window on the side of the barn, lifting the bar on the shutters. He ducked under the window to the other side, and flung the shutter wide open. The loud smack of the wooden shutter diverted the man's attention from the middle of the barn to the window. Coop's rifle was already lined up on the wagon and when the man rose to fire, the old Ranger nailed him in the chest. The man slammed straight backward and toppled into the wagon bed behind the seat, like so much cordwood.

Coop grinned, "May be slower now, but still smarter than most."

He barred the side window and moved back to the front of the barn just in time to blast another Farnum rider off his horse.

* *

Ranger Jim Farley held the rear of the house. He broke silence with, "Thought that you could sneak up the back way, huh?" He fired his Winchester. The man fell as if he were hit with a heavy hammer.

Three more riders streaked around to the back of the house only to find flame, gunsmoke, and hot lead waiting for them. Suddenly, a fullisade of bullets smacked into the window frame where Ranger Farley stood. He ducked quickly, taking a deep breath, and exhaling with a rush.

"Damn them guys! I need some quick help in here!"

Mary Sumner heard Farley yell, and with no immediate target rushed through the house, holding her skirts as she ran. She flattened herself against the opposite wall from the Ranger. Fast movement and excitement left her breathless. Farley looked toward her and uttered, "I shore hope you can shoot as good as you cook, Ma'am."

"Not really, but we'll give them something to think about."

Farley grinned wryly and responded to the woman, "O.K., on the count of three. Both of us will fire at those bushes to the right. Ready? One-two-three!"

Both Jim Farley and Mary Sumner let loose with a barrage of gunfire into the bushes, emptying both of their guns, round after round, in rapid succession.

Two wounded men rolled from the bushes attempting to crawl away. The third man jumped up quickly, firing three bullets at the window before running to his horse.

Farley dropped the empty Winchester Rifle to draw his right hand Colt Revolver. He lined up on the fleeing man, shooting him squarely in the back. The hired gunman pitched forward and rolled to the left.

Meanwhile, Mary Sumner calmly reloaded the Colt Navy. Jim Farley grinned at her as he affirmed his appreciation, "You'll do! Thanks for the help. You better get back to your window now."

* *

Charles Farnum held Cole Stockton's eyes. The two men were momentarily locked in a gaze of hell burning fire. Both men glared at each other with determination and steeled nerves.

Stockton recognized the wild crazy look of madness in Charles Farnum's face. There was only one way to take him and Cole steeled his mind against the pain that he knew was coming. He took his first step toward Farnum, cocking both Colts as he moved.

In the next instant, Cole Stockton began his deadly walk toward his wild-eyed adversary. He fired one Colt after the other as he walked forward.

The old gunman knew what was happening. He was awestruck. He lined his Colt up on Stockton and squeezed off. He saw the sudden impact of his bullet strike Stockton in the left side. A patch of crimson immediately spread along Stockton's shirt.

Stockton grunted with the hit, and dropped his left hand revolver. Farnum took a heavy breath, and then screamed at Cole Stockton. "I am going to kill you!"

He raised his revolver and pointed it directly at Stockton, taking careful aim. He fired the gun only to hear his round smack into the Sumner house wall. Delirious with hate, Farnum shook with rage and fired again and again.

Cole Stockton's mind instantly flashed to the words of his old friend, Wild Bill Hickok, "Take careful aim and shoot the man dead."

Cole Stockton stood deathly still, like a duelist. Charles Farnum's bullets whizzed all around him. He cocked his right hand Colt, turned sideways, took careful aim and squeezed the trigger.

Stockton's bullet struck the demented man in the forehead to exit the back of his skull. He jerked back instantly, and then stood ghastly still for a long moment. His eyes rolled up and his jaw slacked open. His arms hung limply at his side, the smoking Colt Revolver pointed straight down. A nerve tightened and the Colt discharged into the ground in a shower of dirt.

Farnum hovered there for an instant before his knees buckled sending him to the dirt with a thud. Charles Farnum, alias Abner Stokely, the man who professed to perfect the fast draw, was dead.

Those who witnessed the action could not believe what had just happened. Stockton had deliberately walked in on the man with both Colts ready, taking lead himself as though it didn't matter if he lost his life.

Farnum may have perfected the fast draw, but he did not get to use it. His gun had been at the ready, but he faced a man who was willing to sacrifice himself to see justice done.

An eerie silence hung over the Sumner farm. No more rounds were fired. Gunsmoke drifted on the warm air current. Both attackers and defenders alike lowered their weapons and moved into the front yard.

The silence was broken with the thunder of a company of Texas Rangers boiling into the Sumner farmyard. The raiders saw how futile the situation was. Each man dropped his weapons and raised his hands.

Within minutes came the loud bawling of a stampede from the Southwest. Mounted Rangers rode quickly toward the boiling herd, firing their rifles into the air. The frantic steers changed direction and, with the wildly riding Rangers, began to mill aimlessly in a circle. They slowed to a gradual walk.

Laura made her way up to Cole and slipped her arm around his waist. She looked down. "Cole, you've been shot— again. You're bleeding."

"Yes, I know. It looks like your father has another patient, but right now I have something to do."

Cole Stockton reached into his inside vest pocket and pinned on the silver star of a United States Marshal. He walked over to the lifeless body of Charles Farnum and looked down on him. He reached into his own shirt pocket to take out the telegraph order for two thousand dollars, placed it in Farnum's shirt pocket.

He stepped back a bit and stated loudly, "Paid in Full. Delivered and sworn to by a federal officer of the law."

Laura Sumner breathed a long sigh of relief. She looked deeply into Cole Stockton's eyes.

"How can I ever thank you?"

"I'm sure that we will find a way. Right now, let's get something cooking on the stove. A day like this makes a man as hungry as an ole grizzly."

Laura slipped her arms around Cole Stockton and as their lips met, the warmth of the *Lady from Colorado* rekindled the eternal fires of a smoldering bond between the lady and her best friend.

Chapter Seventeen

Smokey Joe Walker

The Overland stagecoach fairly slid to a dust-swirling halt in front of the Express office that served as the stagecoach depot at Denver, Colorado. The main passenger hotel stood next door.

The Denver station agent opened the door of the coach and a handsomely dressed gentleman stepped down to the wooden platform. The man appeared to be middle aged. He wore a suit, dark Stetson, and a vest that sported a gold watch on a chain. A well worn gunbelt sat comfortably around his slim waist.

The gentleman turned to offer his hand to the attractive lady behind him as she stepped out of the coach. She was dressed in a green traveling suit. Her ivory blouse with ruffles was buttoned at the neck, with a dark green velvet tab under an ivory broach.

The young woman's dark hair was coiffed neatly at the nape of her neck to hold a stylish green felt hat. Her crystal blue eyes shined with excitement and wonder. This was her first trip to Denver. She was fascinated by the grandeur before her.

The couple moved away from the coach and stood in quiet conversation. They watched as the hostlers changed out six horse teams. The coach would depart shortly for a return trip to the lower Colorado wilds. Station workers unloaded the luggage from the coach placing it on the boardwalk in front of the hotel.

A hotel porter gathered up their luggage and the couple followed him into the lobby. They would get rooms to rest for the night. In the early morning, they would board the train for the Golden West. San Francisco was their ultimate destination.

The desk clerk smiled a warm greeting as the couple signed the register. He swiveled the large book around to examine the signatures, Bob Cole and Laura Sumner.

"Mr. Cole and Miss Sumner, we are very glad that you chose our establishment for your night's lodging. We offer excellent dining facilities straight through that archway. One of Denver's finest saloons is through the batwings to the left, Sir. There are, of course, other fine restaurants in Denver. I would be happy to recommend some should you desire. Mr. Cole, you are in Room 210 and, Miss Sumner, you are in Room 209. Please enjoy your stay."

The desk clerk handed them their keys and the porter led the way up the stairs with their luggage in tow.

The man registered as Bob Cole opened the door to his room and looked over the accommodations. It was small, but comfortably furnished. He left his valise on the floor at the foot of the bed, then stepped across the hall to Laura Sumner's room. He tipped the porter and closed the door, turning to take her in his arms.

"Well, Laura, here we are in Denver. Is it anything like you imagined?"

"Oh, Cole, it's much more than I envisioned. I'm so glad that you talked me into this vacation. I've always wanted to ride the train, and most of all, I've dreamed of visiting San Francisco. This is most exciting."

"Laura, if you wish, why don't you take a short nap? Later, perhaps about six o'clock, we'll get cleaned up, and have dinner down in the hotel dining room. We must turn in early so we will be fresh for the train ride in the morning."

Cole Stockton, otherwise known as Bob Cole on this trip, shut Laura's door behind him and decided to go to the lobby to pick up a Denver newspaper. As he paid for the paper, he overheard loud laughing and cajoling remarks coming from the saloon. Curiosity led him to have a peek through the swinging doors.

A man with a white beard dressed in worn clothes stood at the bar surrounded by several younger men dressed in suits and ties. Most of the men were laughing at him. He heard the old man say, "But, fellers, I swear that it is true. I do know personally some almighty famous gunfighters. I know'd the likes of Bill Hickock, Clay Allison, Cole Younger, Wes Hardin, Ben Thompson, and Cole Stockton. Why, I even rode a trail or two with some of them."

Cole grinned and chuckled under his breath. The old man was telling some mighty tall tales and most folks would just buy him a whiskey or two to hear his stories and pass it off. Cole had never seen the man before in his life.

He was about to turn away, when one of the men roughly knocked the drink from the old man's hand and pushed him back against the bar.

"You're lying! You don't know any of those men. They wouldn't give you the time of day, you old coot. Get out of this saloon right now, or I'll give you a shooting lesson you won't easily forget."

The angry man reached under his coat and produced a pistol, pointing it at the old man who braced himself against the bar quite shaken with this turn of events. He obviously feared for his life.

Another of the young men turned to the fellow with the pistol and said, "Aw, Terrence, Smokey Joe don't mean no harm. He's just old and likes a whiskey or two now and then. It is not like he was really bragging about himself now. He does know some whoppers, though."

"I don't care!" growled Terrence. "I'm tired of hearing his lies about knowing those men. Those stories are for kids and old folks. If I want to know about those men, I'll waste my money on a good dime novel. I'll bet that none of them are really as fast as they are made out to be. I'd stake my life on it. Why, I'm probably faster than any of them."

Cole Stockton took a deep breath, shook his head and stepped through the bat wing doors. "Why don't you just put that pistol away and cool yourself?" came the firm words.

Terrence turned his head to look at the soft spoken intruder. He looked the newcomer in the dark suit up and down, then sneered, responding, "Why don't you make me. You look like you're packing iron. You think you're good enough to take me?"

The old storyteller looked at the newcomer with apprising eyes. He indeed had seen several gunfighters in his day and he closely took in the manner in which this newcomer wore his gunbelt. He couldn't place the face, but he knew that this man was not someone to trifle with.

"Well, Mister, I'd say that you have about two seconds to drop that pistol before I get real mad. And, you wouldn't like me when I'm mad."

Terrence turned to point his pistol toward the newcomer, to give this intruder his full attention. He stopped in mid movement. His face turned ashen and he suddenly felt sick to his stomach. The pistol dropped to the floor with a thud as Terrence raised his empty hands.

The gentleman, in one fluid movement, had swept his coat back, flashed to his holster, drew the deadly Colt, cocked the hammer back and had it leveled straight at Terrence's midsection. The entire action was an instant blur to those who tried to follow it. The onlookers stood along the bar, mouths open and eyes wide. They had never seen a faster draw.

"Now then, that's more like it. I suggest that if you don't like Smokey Joe's stories, you turn and leave. As for myself, I would enjoy listening and learning. I believe that you owe for a spilled whiskey—not to mention a bit more for your rudeness. You will, of course, buy a round of drinks for your company and then quietly depart—with apologies to all. That is, unless you would like to pick up that peashooter and step out into the street. Then, we could do this for real."

"Who are you?" asked one of the men.

"Just someone who likes a good story now and then and hates to see folks picked on."

Terrence lowered one hand to his pocket and produced a wallet. He ordered a round of drinks, and leaving his pistol lying on the plank floor, quickly left the saloon. The others enjoyed another story along with a glass of whiskey.

The stranger stayed for the story, and thanked Smokey Joe, before taking his newspaper up to his room for a rest.

One of the young men inquired, "Smokey Joe, who was that man? Do you know who he is? My God, did you see that? Terrence started to turn and that man's gun was in his hand faster than my eyes could follow."

Smokey Joe could only mutter, "My friends, I have seen many gunmen in my time. His face is familiar, but I can't place that man. I will tell you one thing, though, he is a man to reckon with. I sure wish I knew just who he is."

* *

Seven o'clock in the evening found Cole and Laura enjoying a beefsteak dinner in the hotel dining room. Laura's excitement brought her to chatter throughout the meal. Her anticipation of the train ride and what San Francisco might be like were exhilarating. Her eyes sparkled.

Cole was amused with Laura's thoughts. He decided to give her a more realistic vision of rail coach travel. "Well, Laura, the train ride will be more comfortable than the stagecoach. There is more room to move around in your seat. It won't be as dusty; however, the smoke from the engine might irritate your eyes and leave soot on your jacket. The trip will still be long, but you can get up to stretch your legs by walking up and down the aisle. There will be a lot of new country to see and, I might add, some interesting characters."

"Cole, you know that I don't mind the discomforts. I have heard and read much about the Golden West, and now we are on our way to enjoy it."

"There is one more thing, Laura. As always, there may be dangers associated with this train ride. There are robbers, Indians, accidents, and the like. I would feel most comfortable if you kept your Colt Lightning handy in your handbag and not in your valise. You can never tell what might come up."

"So, that is why you asked me to bring it? Is there something that you haven't told me about this trip?"

"I just want you to be prepared. Don't worry about anything."

Laura had no intention of allowing worry to spoil her grand adventure. She smiled contentedly.

* *

Unknown to Cole and Laura, cold eyes watched them from a distance. Terrence Whatley sat in an obscure corner of the dining room. He observed the couple with a burning dislike for the man who had embarrassed him in the saloon and interfered in his business.

Whatley planned to ride the train toward the West in the morning along with three others of his gang. When the time was right, while the train was slowly climbing the crest of a long grade, even more of his group would emerge from the trees and board the train. Their objective was the Express Car, which carried gold shipments.

The plan seemed perfect. After all, they had robbed four trains in the past months and no one had found them out. Their group included a major contact with the primary Colorado Springs mine that shipped gold bullion, as well as a highly compensated Wells Fargo employee. Word came from their informants that a large gold shipment was moving on this train. Terrence and his organization would relieve Wells Fargo of that shipment. Nothing would stand in their way.

Whatley mentally rehearsed their plan. Each train passenger car would have at least one gang member aboard to keep passengers in line while three of their men in the first passenger car would place a dynamite charge against the Express Car and blow the rear door off. They would dash inside and subdue the Wells Fargo Express agents before opening the side loading door and shoving the strong boxes out. All this would happen while the train moved slowly up the mountain grade. Terrence knew the importance of the timing of this heist. A gang member, holding horses for each man when the job was done, would allow for a quick escape.

Terrence knew the gang had become notorious. Lawmen from all over sought to arrest the outlaws. This would be Terrence's last job with the gang. He would take his share along with the money he had stashed from the previous jobs and go back East. He would lose himself in a large city like Chicago or even New York City. He could become a gentleman of leisure, without worry of money for a long time.

Just now, his thoughts returned to the tall, lanky intruder. He would take care of this man at the same time. "I don't know who that man is, nor do I care. No one interferes in my business like that and gets away with it."

* *

The first rays of the morning sun peeked over the city of Denver from the east. Already, there was bustling activity at the rail station. An Overland stagecoach stood next to the Express Car and heavily armed Wells Fargo guards stood watch as several men passed heavy iron boxes through the doorway. Another man, tall and lanky, stood on the platform and observed the activity, too.

When the Wells Fargo men were finished with their task, John Dunne, Chief Special Agent for the Wells Fargo Company, walked up to the observer.

"Well, Marshal Stockton, there it is. The boxes are loaded just as we discussed. There will be two Express guards inside the car. They will open the door for no one except you. This railroad line has been plagued with robberies for the past several months. I think that there is an information leak somewhere within the company. The gang seems to know just when, where, and how much is being shipped. I sure hope you know what you are doing."

"Thank you, John. I think that everything will be all right. Now, you can see to the other arrangements that we discussed. Are you sure that you spoke to none of your employees about it?"

"Yes, Sir. The only ones who know right now are you and I. I'll start the next phase of our plan just as soon as this train pulls out."

* *

Cole Stockton took leave of the train station and walked briskly back to the hotel. He rapped lightly on Laura's door and smiled warmly when she opened it. She was dressed in a deep blue traveling suit with ruffled blouse. Her dark hair was held back with a matching ribbon, allowing it to tumble softly on her shoulders. Her eyes shined with excitement.

They walked down to the lobby with their valises in hand, setting them on the floor while they checked out. They turned to the door when the familiar figure of Smokey Joe stood up from a wicker chair just outside on the porch.

"Good morning, Sir. I didn't get a chance to thank you last night and I thought that I would wait until you came down this morning. I sure wish that I knew who you remind me of. Maybe I will find out in time."

Cole replied with a smile. "That's all right, Smokey Joe. Don't let it bother you. We have to get to the rail station. Take care of yourself now."

Not really understanding the reference to "last night," Laura looked questioningly at Cole, but his mind focused on getting to the train station. She put aside her question for later.

Cole and Laura boarded the waiting wagon, and when all the passengers were seated, the coach rumbled to the station. Laura Sumner turned to look at Cole.

"Who was that old man, Cole? What did he mean about thanking you?"

"Oh, I guess that he was pleased that I listened to his stories and tall tales about famous gunfighters last night. He can sure tell some whoppers. Why, he is even better than those dime novels that I've read."

Laura wasn't completely convinced that Cole had told her the whole story about the old man, but she didn't feel the need to press him for answers.

* *

Smokey Joe pondered the situation. He was extremely curious about the identity of the quick drawing stranger. He thought about how much money he had stashed away for rainy days and made his decision.

"By George, I'm gonna follow that man and find out just who he is. Maybe I can find out more stories if I follow him. He's mysterious enough, and the way he handles that six-gun, he's sure exciting to watch. That woman is some kind of pleasing to my tired old eyes as well. Yes, sir, it's about time to travel a bit. Be good for my soul."

Smokey Joe hurried down to his shanty behind the livery stables and, opening the loose boards, retrieved the small leather pouch of coins. He stuffed a few of his possibles into a small, worn satchel. Turning toward the door, he stopped for a moment. As a last minute thought, he dug into an old trunk and produced an early model Colt Frontier Revolver and a box of cartridges. He stuffed the ammunition into a coat pocket, and slipped the revolver into his belt.

Smokey Joe then made his way quickly to the rail stationhouse where he bought a ticket to the end of the line—San Francisco.

Chapter Eighteen

Ribbons of Steel

Arriving at the Denver rail station in a carriage from the hotel, Cole Stockton and Laura Sumner observed that their scheduled train was being prepared for departure. Cole had already obtained their tickets earlier that morning. Now they stepped out onto the rail station platform to join other ticketed passengers who were viewing the impressive steam engine and the line of rail cars. The train consisted of the steam locomotive, a tender car piled high with blocks of cut wood, a baggage car, an Express car, and three passenger cars, sometimes referred to as coaches.

The engineer and brakemen performed last minute checks of the locomotive and rail cars. Porters pushed carts of luggage and consigned freight along the platform to the baggage car where workmen loaded it into the baggage car.

When time came to board the train, the conductor announced the impending departure. Passengers lined up beside their selected passenger cars and began to board. Porters assisted ladies in boarding.

Cole guided Laura to the rear most passenger car of the Denver and Rio Grande Railway train. He helped her up the steps and, upon entering the car, indicated that they should take the last row of seats on the right side.

Cole explained, "I like the last row out of habit, I suppose. That's so that I can take stock of all the travelers in the coach." He didn't mention that he could also watch who entered the railcar from the front as well as who might suddenly appear from the rear of the train from those seats.

Laura was fascinated with the interior of the rail passenger car. Just inside the front entrance, there sat a pot bellied stove with a metal box filled with kindling for cold weather. There were rows of wooden seats separated by an aisle down the center. She noticed what appeared to be a small closet at the rear entrance to the car and remarked about it.

"Look, Cole, they put a closet in here to hang up your coat."

Cole smiled and then announced in a gentle voice, "Laura, that closet is actually a toilet for the call of nature." He watched as her eyes widened. Having never traveled on the railroad before, she had no idea what accommodations were available in the passenger rail cars.

Only a few more minutes had passed when two rough looking men wearing long coats entered their passenger car. Looking around, one man took the seat opposite Cole and Laura. The other man took a position in the first row of seats at the front of the coach. He was right beside the doorway to the passenger car in front of theirs.

It wasn't long before the conductor came through the rail car to take tickets. Once done, he stepped outside the rear of the train and waved toward the engineer who was watching for his signal. "All Aboard! All Aboard!" cried out the conductor.

The train ride began with a hard jerk forward, spinning solid iron wheels, the blast of a whistle, and the clanging of bells. A long column of dark wood smoke trailed back from the engine and there was the distinct odor of burning pine. The ride had begun.

Cole pondered these last two men who boarded. Something deep within told him that they warranted considerable watching. They had boarded together, but now sat at opposite ends of the coach.

* *

Smokey Joe watched the mystery man board the last passenger car with his lady. He decided to remain in the shadows and boarded the second passenger car to take a seat at the rear entrance. He settled down for the trip. The old fellow was amused with himself that he would make a decision to travel so quickly.

Smokey surveyed the situation. He was riding the same train as that mysterious man. At each stop, he planned to follow this man until he found out just who he was. Smokey Joe glanced over the passengers in his coach. A familiar figure boarded the car and sat alone at the opposite end, reading a newspaper—Terrence Whatley.

"I wonder what he's doing on this train?" pondered the old man as he nestled himself low into the corner of his seat. He would have liked traveling better without the likes of that no-good Terrence Whatley.

* *

Miles and miles of steel track guided the chugging engine as it made its way through passes, winding its way through the Rocky Mountains.

Gradually, the train slowed considerably as it began the ascent up a long grade. Laura sat looking out the window, watching the beauty of the landscape slip past.

Cole's instinct told him that something was about to happen. He watched the man in the front of the passenger car more intensely. He seemed nervous about something.   Cole leaned toward Laura and spoke softly, "Laura, I'm going to walk casually toward the front of this rail car. I want you to watch that gent across from us. Should he reach under his coat, be ready to shoot fast. Watch the door behind us as well."

Suddenly, Laura became alert to danger. She was no longer a sightseer. Carefully, she nodded and reached for her purse and the Colt Lighting.

Cole stood, stretched, and moved into the aisle. As he took his first steps toward the front of the car, the man at the far end jumped out of his seat, threw open his coat and reached for his gun.

Passengers on the rail car jerked to life with the sudden movement. A woman screamed. Other passengers flung themselves onto the floor between the seats, where they huddled in fear.

Stockton's right hand swept to his holster. The Colt fairly leaped into his hand. In one fluid movement it rose, cocked, and leveled at the man with the gun in his hand. The Colt bucked in Cole's hand, and the man slammed back against the forward wall, his own revolver just barely clearing his holster and firing wild. The bullet smacked into the floor at mid-coach.

A male passenger crouched between the seats blurted out, "Oh my God!" as splinters spewed up before his fearful eyes.

Laura watched intently as the unsavory character across from her reached into his coat. His hand withdrew the blackened steel of a revolver. With practiced hand, she quickly drew her own Colt Lightning and shot the man in his middle.

He jerked back against the seat with a surprised look on his bearded face. He glanced down at his chest to see the red stain spread across his shirt. He attempted to raise his own weapon to line on the determined looking woman.

Laura had already cocked her revolver for the second time and was squeezing the trigger. The second bullet spun out of the barrel amid a sharp crack, burst of flame, and blackened powder smoke.

The man grunted, and then fell backward against the window. His weapon slipped from his right hand and fell with a thud to the floor of the railcar.

Cole walked cautiously up to the fallen man. He was dead. He turned and announced to the passengers. "U.S. Marshal! This train is being robbed! I want you to stay down where you are. There may be more gunfire."

* *

Lloyd Jackson, the main Wells Fargo express guard, heard the rolling crackle of gunfire from the passenger coaches. He turned to his fellow express guard, Lem Sutter, and told him to be ready for action. The two men readied their shotguns.

The incessant clacking of the train on the rails seemed deafening. Without warning, an explosion tore out the rear door of the express car. Within moments, two armed men with masks burst into the car, firing as they came.

Jackson fell, shot through the right side and lay still. Sutter was killed outright.

The outlaws moved rapidly. They threw open the loading door of the express car, dragged the iron boxes to the opening, and threw them out one by one as the train moved slowly along the grade.

Afterward, one by one, the two masked men jumped out of the car, rolling with the momentum. Once on their feet again, they scrambled toward the iron boxes of gold bullion.

* *

Smokey Joe heard the crackle of gunfire from the rear of the train. The shots brought Terrence Whatley to his feet. With a smirk on his face, the no-good rose and reached under his coat to a shoulder holster for his short-barreled Colt Revolver.

Other passengers saw Terrence's movements. They quickly glanced around the passenger coach to see Terrence draw a weapon in front of them and Smokey Joe draw a gun behind them.

Smokey Joe realized what was happening. He reached to his belt to draw his Colt. "Terrence!" he shouted, "drop that gun or I'll drill you."

There were muffled screams as the other passengers threw themselves between the seats of the railcar for as much protection as they could get.

Whatley, startled by the challenge, could not believe his eyes. No! It could not be the old storyteller.

Smokey Joe faced him from behind the last row of seats with a revolver in his hands. The revolver wavered a mite.

Terrence grinned crookedly. "Hey, old man! You can't even hold that gun steady. I'll bet you can't even shoot it straight."

Terrence leveled his own pistol at the old man and cocked it. "Old man," he roared, "I'm going to rid the world of your tall tales and lies. I'm going to shoot you right between the eyes and put you out of your misery."

With Whatley's last statement, Smokey Joe pounced into the aisle snarling like a cougar. His feet spread apart. He crouched low, the revolver in his right hand and his left palm fanning the hammer as fast as he could.

Three sharp cracks split the air as black powder smoke and flame belched from the Colt.

Whatley's face showed the horror of being hit by three whistling chucks of molten lead. Each one plowed dead center into his chest within a radius of four inches. He jerked backward with each hit to slam against the forward wall of the rail car. He glared at the old man who slowly approached him, the still-smoking Colt in his hand.

"You—you—you shot me. I never thought you could be—so—fast."

His words trailed off as Terrence Whatley paid the ultimate price for underestimating his adversary—his life.

Smokey Joe stood looking down at the dead man. He shook his head. "A skill I learned from Wild Bill. But, you never listened to my story. That's too bad. Now, I got to get to the front of this here train and see what's going on. I'll bet the mystery man had something to do with that gunfire behind us. He may need some help and I'm of the mind to do it."

Joe stepped over the body, and out onto the platform of the first passenger coach. He peered through the window of the coach's rear door. Two armed men stood at the front of the coach with weapons drawn. Smokey returned to the second passenger coach to consider his next move.

"Holy Smokes! The train's being robbed!" announced Smokey Joe to the cowering passengers.

He reached down and took Terrence Whatley's revolver from his lifeless hand. "I might just need this one, too. He ain't got no more use for it."

Smokey Joe leaped from the second passenger car onto the rear of the first passenger car. As he opened the door and dashed inside, he was met with bullets smacking into the walls around him. The two outlaws holding passengers at bay were about to make their escape and jump off the train.

Joe made a quick appraisal and began to fire hot lead into the midst of the duo. They dived quickly into the seat areas on either side of the aisle.

Smokey Joe hunkered down in the last row of seats before the rear bulkhead of the coach. He shouted, "Come and get it boys! I got plenty for yah!" He methodically fired the two revolvers to keep the bandits pinned down.

Female passengers screamed with fear, and male passengers swore loudly as the forward passenger rail car became a battleground between Smokey Joe and the two outlaws.

* *

Cole Stockton had started through the forward door of the third railcar when the sudden explosion from the end of the express car shook the train. He stumbled off balance and fell backward on top of some shocked passengers.

The sudden jolt rocked Laura Sumner back against the wall of their coach. She slammed forward again, against the seat in front of her. She slipped to the floor between the seats.

Stockton staggered around and finally managed to get to his feet. His Colt was somewhere on the floor amongst the pile of passengers.

He reached behind his back and drew his second revolver. He glanced out the window of the coach to see iron boxes roll down the rail grade. Masked men then followed, rolling with the momentum, and came up scrambling toward the strongboxes.

"Damn it!" he uttered under his breath.

Crackles of gunfire sounded from the front of the train. Cole sprang back into action. He moved cautiously forward to open the front door of the rail car. He stopped to look at Laura who waved him off, acknowledging that she was all right.

Stockton moved through the door and leaped onto the landing of the second passenger car. He burst into the rear of the car with revolver at the ready. Aside from timid passengers chancing a peek over the backs of seats, a single body lay sprawled in the aisle at the front of the car.

He loudly announced himself, "U.S. Marshal! Stay where you are! There will be more shooting."

Cole moved forward and examined the body. It was Terrence Whatley. He wondered, "What was Terrence doing on this train?"

Gunfire resounded steadily from the railcar in front of him. Cole moved onto the platform of the first passenger rail car. He crouched low and, grabbing the door handle, he swung it open and dived through to hit the floor.

Deep furrows splintered the walls and aisle floor as hot lead whistled through the air. He rolled to the right to position himself behind the rear set of seats.

Stockton glanced across the aisle and found himself looking straight at a grinning Smokey Joe. "Glad you could join us," cackled the old man, "Thought that I'd have to keep these guys pinned down all by my lonesome. What did you say your name was?"

"Oh, all right. I'm Cole Stockton, United States Marshal."

"Lord Almighty! I should have known. They ain't many as fast as you."

"We'll talk about it later. Right now, let's smoke these guys out. Give me a minute to reload. Can you hold them, Smokey?"

"You got it, Cole. All right, boys, drop your guns or grab for harps! We're coming to get you."

The two men at the front of the coach were dumbfounded. The old man stood and along with him was the man who had dived into the car. Each moved toward them with guns blazing.

Bullets whined though the air all around the robbers. Splinters flew as each of the men grabbed parts of his body for protection. They resembled porcupines.

The outlaws huddled on the floor of the coach, holding an arm over their faces as they attempted to pull splinters from one another.

As quickly as it had begun, the firing stopped. The gang members peered up into the deadly bores of three Colt Revolvers, cocked and ready. A voice spoke quietly, "U.S. Marshal! Drop your guns and crawl out of those seats."

"And," came the gravelly second voice, "be mighty careful of how you crawl. I got an itchy trigger finger."

Cole turned to Smokey Joe. "Joe, watch these two for me. I've got to check on the express guards and stop this train."

Joe looked at the two sullen prisoners and remarked, "Hear that, boys? I'm gonna watch you guys. Please don't make no sudden moves. My old trigger finger might slip and then you would get hurt real bad."

Stockton left the two prisoners in Smokey Joe's capable hands. Opening the door, he hesitated a moment as he surveyed the magnitude of the blast to the express car. He made his way into the wreckage to find the express guard Sutter sprawled dead on the floor. Lloyd Jackson was alive, but wounded. He lay groaning in a corner. Cole bent down to check Jackson, who indicated that he was all right and waved Cole onward.

Stockton exited the opposite side of the express car and into the baggage car. Everything there seemed intact. Then, he moved out the baggage car front door and onto the tender car. Climbing over the tender, he encountered the engineer and two firemen who looked up in astonishment. The firemen started toward him with shovels raised as if to strike down the intruder.

"Hold it, boys!" exclaimed Cole "U.S. Marshal! The train was boarded from behind and robbed. I want you to stop the train and back up—slowly, until I tell you to stop."

"Yes, sir, Marshal!" came the response of the engineer. He shifted gears and applied the brake. The heavy iron wheels reversed and began to spin on the tracks. The train slid to a momentary halt before it backed up slowly.

Cole stood in the cabin of the engine and watched the landscape as the train gained momentum. The train moved much faster going down the grade than the long pull uphill.

Finally, he saw what he was looking for—the strong boxes. The train robbers had shot the locks off the boxes to get at the gold shipment. A silly grin spread across his face.

"O.K., engineer, stop the train! We'll wait right here. Immediately make sure that someone is posted at the rear of the train with hazard lanterns. There is another unscheduled train coming up behind us. It should be here within the next thirty minutes."

Stockton returned to the express car to survey the damage. Express agent Jackson was sitting up, but needed medical attention. Cole pressed a compress of his handkerchief into Jackson's side.

"Marshal Stockton, we sure didn't think they would blow the door off the end of the express car. Everything happened so fast that we were helpless. They got the boxes. I sure hope that you catch those guys. Lem was my best friend."

Cole replied, "We'll get them all, and soon. I have two of them up in the first passenger car, thanks to a new friend of mine. Chief Special Agent John Dunne will arrive shortly on the train behind us. He has horses and a handpicked posse to track down those men. You rest easy now. We will get you to a doctor as quickly as we can. Can you stand? I want to move you to the passenger coach where my friend Laura will help you."

Jackson stammered, "I can walk, with some help."

Stockton assisted the wounded agent to the passenger coach. Laura asked another woman who offered her medical training to help tend to Agent Jackson.

Cole turned to Laura. "Laura, there's a posse coming up behind us. I'm going to ride with them for a few hours. I want you to stay on the train. Continue traveling toward San Francisco. I will catch up as soon as I can."

All right, Cole. Come here." She put her arms around him and kissed him. "That's just to let you know that I'll miss you—even for a few hours. Bring those men in, Cole."

Chapter Nineteen

Pursuit of the Train Robbers

The special second train slid to a grinding halt some thirty yards behind the regular scheduled train. Wells Fargo Chief Special Agent, John Dunne, was in the engine. He leaped to the ground once the train stopped and immediately shouted orders to twelve men who rode a flatcar piled with saddles, rifles, and packs. The men began to unload horses from the stock car behind the flatbed. Stockton and Dunne met midway between the trains.

"Well, Cole, it looks like they took the bait. You know, I'd like to see their faces when they open those satchels and find them rocks. Someone will have hell to pay."

"I'm counting on it, John. They will no doubt go directly to the informant—to express their deep displeasure. I'm hoping that we can be around when it comes about. O.K., let's get our posse moving. I want to see where they're headed."

U.S. Marshal Cole Stockton, Chief Special Agent Dunne, and twelve Wells Fargo men rode off following the tracks left by the train robbers.

* *

Henry Tuttle, a man with a thin face and balding head, was slightly stooped from the many years of toiling over ledgers and documents. Tuttle was the clerk at the Denver Wells Fargo Express Office. This particular evening, he stayed late at his desk in order to finish his work. Interruptions during the day had put him behind on the task of reviewing each invoice.

Henry sat at his roll top desk pondering the pile of invoices. The more he examined them, the more puzzled he became. Something was not right. He checked them again and again. When he placed two side by side, he found it.

"Now, why are there two copies of this gold shipment advisory. There's only supposed to be one. Someone made an unauthorized copy. I wonder why?"

Just then the door opened and Joel Pierce, the mining company foreman, walked in and closed the door behind him. He looked distressed. He peered cautiously at the middle aged clerk, then asked, "Is Mr. Nettleton in his office?"

Samuel Nettleton was the Denver Wells Fargo Agent in charge.

Henry looked up over his wire-rimmed spectacles and replied, "I think that he may be over at the Double Eagle saloon. He usually stops in there for a drink or two before he goes home for the evening. Can I help you with something?"

"No, Tuttle. I have an important matter to discuss with him. I'll walk over to the saloon and he better be there."

Tuttle frowned. He didn't care for Pierce. The man was a bully. Rumor had it that he was particularly hard on his mineworkers as well.

Minutes ticked by as Tuttle meticulously worked his figures. Suddenly, both Pierce and Nettleton burst through the door.

Nettleton looked worried. He turned to Tuttle and instructed him to close up shop and go home. He could work his files another night. The two men abruptly went into the station agent's office, slamming the door behind them. Tuttle could hear muffled words as he slipped out of the door to walk toward the boarding house where he lived.

Tuttle was within two doors of the boarding house when shots cracked through the stillness of the night. He turned to look back at the Wells Fargo Express Office and saw Pierce run out with a satchel, mount his horse and spur out of town like the very devil himself was on his heels.

A grim vision came to Tuttle. He dashed for the Express Office. He found both the front door and the station agent's office wide open. Tuttle moved to the doorway of Nettleton's office and peered inside.

Samuel Nettleton lay face down in a pool of blood. His private safe was open and papers lay scattered over the room.

"I've got to get the law," exclaimed Tuttle. He dashed out to the dusty street shouting for help. It was then that he recognized Agent Dunne among a group of riders headed toward him. He flung his arms frantically to get his attention.

Quickly, Tuttle explained what he had heard and seen. Chief Agent Dunne turned to Cole Stockton to offer an opinion.

"Cole, it looks like Nettleton was the informant. Both he and Pierce appear to have been together in this. Pierce must have killed him for whatever share that Nettleton had stashed. He's probably on his way out of the territory. We can't follow him in the dark. I'll take the posse and pick up his trail in the morning. Why don't you ride on to catch that train? I know a lovely woman who is waiting to see you."

Cole replied, "John, I sure hate to turn back now. Pierce has only about a half an hour's start on us. But, you're right. It's too dark to follow. Those other three gents, had they not decided to shoot it out, might have got us here quicker. Well, you know what he looks like. Have a wanted poster made up on him and post it all over the Territory. Someone is bound to want some reward money. I'll go catch that train. Laura and I are sure looking forward to some peace and quiet in San Francisco."

* *

The posse train followed the scheduled train until they reached a side switch rail, where the damaged rail cars were coupled with the second engine. The scheduled train with its passenger cars continued the journey toward Salt Lake City.

Behind schedule, the train chugged in darkness, winding its way toward Utah and points west. Laura Sumner reclined in her seat. She was weary from the emotion of the robbery and tried to get some rest. It had been an eventful day.

She thought of Cole Stockton. He was somewhere out there with that posse tracking down the remainder of the train robbers. She wished that he were there with her and a bit of loneliness crept into her mind. She stared out the window of the rail coach.

Laura couldn't see anything in the darkness, but her mind suggested scenes of the bustling city of San Francisco. She and Cole would have a great time—once they got there. At about two o'clock in the morning the train began to slow down.

The conductor walked through the cars and announced that they would stop to take on fuel and water. It would take some thirty minutes. Passengers could get out on the small station platform to stretch their legs if they wished. There would be coffee and sandwiches available in the station house.

Laura decided to get some coffee and perhaps a sandwich. She stepped off the train and entered the station along with a few other passengers. She purchased the coffee and sat on a bench leisurely sipping the strong dark liquid when she noticed a big burly man in dirty rough looking clothes. He was unshaven. He wore a gunbelt like he knew how to use it. The man was purchasing a train ticket.

Ordinarily, she would not have paid much attention, but the man carried an almost new black satchel that didn't match his character. She wondered about him and so decided to move a bit closer. She overheard him ask for a ticket to San Francisco. He would be on the same train.

Laura's curiosity peaked even higher when the man paid for his ticket with a large bill. She decided that she should watch this man.

Minutes passed and the train was finally ready to continue the journey. Laura walked out to the platform and waited her turn to step onto the waiting passenger car. Her eyes followed the burly man's movements. She observed him enter the car behind hers.

"Oh, well," she thought, "maybe it's all right. Still, I feel that there is something about that man—something foreboding. I do wish that Cole were here. I would share what I saw and heard on the platform. No! Cole would more than likely say that I'm just being silly, and that there are lots of rough looking people in the West on their way to San Francisco. I'd better get to my seat. The train is beginning to leave the station."

Laura sat down and made herself comfortable leaning between the seat and the window. She pulled a shawl from her valise and placed it around herself. She had just closed her eyes when the door to the coach opened. The clatter and clacking of the iron wheels along the rails were loud. Someone must have entered the passenger coach. She looked up.

It was the burly man. He moved toward the far end of the car and found an empty seat against the back wall. He settled himself in. He appeared very guarded about the satchel.

Without moving, Laura watched the man. There was something in his manner that she did not like. The more she thought about it, the more the feeling enveloped her. She shivered a bit. When she did finally close her eyes, Laura was lulled to sleep by the dull clacking sound and rocking movement of the train.

Dreams came to the Lady from Colorado. She envisioned Cole Stockton standing before her. He faced that burly man and the man had a gun in his hand. The man had an evil sneer on his face. He fired the gun.

Laura Sumner jerked up wide-eyed from her dream. She looked around. The man was still at the far end of the coach and wide-awake. Their eyes met.

She could feel the penetrating evil of the man's heart. She had to avert her eyes to break the spell. Another icy cold shiver ran through her body.

Chapter Twenty

The Fugitive

Cole Stockton rode through the night. He had a train to catch. It was roughly three o'clock in the morning when he rode into the small rail town and entered the station house. He walked up to the tired looking man at the counter and asked if the train from Denver had gotten there yet.

"You're too late," replied the rail clerk. "The train pulled out about thirty minutes ago. Not another until tomorrow, same time."

Cole thought for moment. "You got a livery in this town? I need a fresh horse. Someone important is on that train, and I've just got to catch up with her."

"Right on down to the end of the street. Bang on the door to the right. The hostler sleeps there. He'll rent you a horse."

Cole rode to the livery and rousted out the hostler. He followed the foul smelling man in rumpled clothes into the building. As he passed the row of stalls, he noticed one horse in particular. The animal had been ridden hard recently. Frothy lather lay caked on withers and flanks of the horse. The rider had not bothered to care for the animal.

"Where did that horse come from?" inquired Stockton.

"Some feller rode him in about an hour and a half ago. He was in a big hurry, too. He said that he had a train to catch."

"What did he look like?" Cole questioned.

"He was a big, ugly feller. Mean looking too. He wore bibbed, mining clothes, jeans and carried a black satchel. Thought it out of the ordinary, but there are a lot of strange looking people here 'bouts. Yeah, and he had the coldest eyes I ever seen. Why do you ask? He a friend of yourn?"

"No, not a friend, but I really need to catch up with this guy. Which is your fastest horse? I'll take it."

"You are going to try and catch that train, aren't you?"

"Yes, I am."

"Well, sir, the fastest way is straight north to the base of the Rockies, then turn west. You should find the train somewhere along the flats."

Stockton inquired, "But that train is heading west. Won't I miss it?"

"Naw!" informed the hostler. The rails wind through the mountain passes. You'll be taking the short way. Right over the pass and down onto the flats. Probably get there way ahead of the train."

"Thanks. Rub down my horse please, and feed it. And, on second thought, do the same for that other mount. Here's two dollars extra for your help." Cole handed the man two silver coins.

Stockton took the saddle off his weary mount and saddled up a powerful looking black gelding with white blazed face. He led it out of the livery then, swung wearily into the saddle. He turned toward the north end of town and heeled its flanks. The horse was game and started with a jump. Within seconds, he was in a full gallop down the street.

Cole's mind raced. Now there was a second reason to catch that train. Joel Pierce was on it.

* *

The darkness began to lighten as the first rays of sunlight touched the peaks of the Rockies. The train moved slowly along the silvery ribbons of steel. Dark wood smoke billowed from its stack and formed a long tail that drifted aimlessly on the soft morning breeze.

The train rounded the final turn to appear at the bottom of the foothills. It moved out onto the flats of Utah. There it picked up speed. Within twenty minutes, the engine would stop at yet another small town to take on fuel and water: the last stop before it reached Salt Lake City.

Laura Sumner looked out the window as the train pulled into the small station. A lone figure stood on the platform near the door of the station. She rubbed her eyes. Could it be? Yes, it was.

Cole Stockton was waiting for the train.

The huge iron wheels spun on the track. Smoke billowed from the stack, and hot steam blew out from the boilers. The train ground to a halt.

Laura picked up her handbag, stood and turned to leave the coach. A gruff voice behind her called out, "What's your hurry, lady. I noticed you looking at me. I may not look like much right now, but I got a lot of money. When we reach San Francisco, I can treat you right—like a real lady."

Laura felt the distaste. "No, thank you. My friend is waiting for me on the platform. Now, if you will excuse me, I will join him."

"Your man—is he from around here, in Utah?"

"No. He is from the Lower Colorado. You may have heard of him. His name is Cole Stockton, and he's the United States Marshal." Just saying his name and title gave Laura such pleasure. The threatening passenger had Cole Stockton to think about now.

Joel Pierce suddenly felt ill at ease. He had heard of Stockton and now he looked out on the platform. Cole Stockton walked toward the passenger car.

Pierce panicked. He drew his revolver and grabbed Laura's arm. He pulled her roughly in front of him.

"You're staying with me. Just keep quiet and your man will live. Say anything and I'll kill him faster than you can wink. I mean what I say." Laura mumbled her understanding.

The door to the passenger coach opened and Stockton entered to find Laura standing at the opposite end of the coach. A burly man in bibbed work jeans stood behind her.

Cole watched Laura's eyes. She glanced down—down toward her handbag. Her right hand was inching into the purse. Stockton issued the warning.

"Let her go, Pierce! You are under arrest for conspiracy, robbery, and murder. Let her go and I'll see you get a fair trial. Harm her and I'll kill you."

"No! You listen up, Mr. Marshal. You try anything and I hurt your woman. I can hurt her bad. You understand?"

Joel Pierce held his revolver in one hand and Laura with the other. He was holding her arm with the same hand that held tightly onto the black satchel.

Laura felt her right hand grasp the butt of her Colt Lightning. She eased it out of the handbag.

Pierce continued to concentrate on Stockton. Suddenly, he heard the metallic click of metal against metal. It definitely was the sound of a revolver hammer cocking back. He looked down at Laura's hand. It held a cocked revolver.

Laura forcefully jerked loose from Pierce and threw herself to the floor of the coach, turning as she fell, to face Pierce. She pointed the gun at him and squeezed the trigger.

Pierce jumped back in surprise. His eyes flashed to Stockton. The man's hand was a blur. He saw the deadly Colt rise out of the holster, a flash of flame, a burst of powder smoke and then the hot lead burned into his chest.

Sharp cracks resounded through the passenger coach as two revolvers spit death and destruction. Pierce jerked back with each bullet, then fell straight back against the wall of the railcar. His eyes were wide with disbelief, and his mouth open.

Both the woman and the man had shot him at the same instant. The dark veil of Hell's Gates opened for his murderous soul as he fell screaming into the pit of Purgatory.

Smokey Joe Walker had decided to stretch his legs on the station platform. He stood up, stretched, and shuffled to the doorway of the passenger car. Gunfire erupted from the forward passenger coach. Smokey Joe dashed ahead and boarded the car while passengers on the platform ducked for cover. No one expected a shootout aboard a waiting train.

Inside the coach, the door to the rail car burst open to admit Smokey Joe, revolver in hand, and eyes shining with determination. He stopped suddenly and lowered his Colt. A wide grin spread across his face.

Cole Stockton had his arms around Laura Sumner as they kissed.

"Well, now! I can see that you two don't need any saving by the likes of ole Smokey Joe. I'll get the local law in here to clean up this mess."

* *

A short time later, the local sheriff and the Wells Fargo agent for the small station boarded the passenger car. Cole identified the deceased, and turned the black satchel over to the agent who announced, "There is a $1,000 dollar reward for this man, Marshal, dead or alive. Who gets it?"

Cole shot a glance toward Laura before he replied, "I guess that Miss Sumner here gets this reward. There is another reward posted for information and capture of others of the gang. See that Mr. Smokey Joe Walker gets that reward. While I'm thinking about it—Smokey Joe is pretty handy with that six-shooter of his. You would do well to hire him to ride the trains to spot outlaws."

* *

The undertaker and the Wells Fargo agent removed the deceased and the money satchel from the train while rail employees refilled wood and water on board.

The big locomotive blew hot steam from its valves, the bell clanged, and the engineer blew the whistle in three loud blasts for yet another station departure. The giant iron wheels began to slip and turn on the steel ribbons. The iron maiden lurched forward. Within minutes, the stack billowed a long trail of dark smoke as the train chugged on its way to Salt Lake City where Cole and Laura would change trains again. This time, the destination was the city of San Francisco.

Cole and Laura sat together once again. She snuggled in his arms as they leaned together with the rocking and swaying of the passenger coach. They slept that way through the night.

A few days later, found the train chugging through the California hills into the panorama of the San Francisco Bay area.

Laura was incredibly excited. "Oh, Cole! It's beautiful. Look at all the ships in the harbor. The ocean, it's s-o-o-o blue. You can see it for miles and miles. I'd bet that it goes at least a hundred miles. I want to walk along the water and see it all."

Cole smiled at her with soft and gentle eyes. "We will, Laura. We will see all of San Francisco."

* *

The carriage from the San Francisco rail station pulled up in front of the Grand Hotel. Porters moved quickly from the building to immediately begin unloading luggage.

Cole Stockton and Laura Sumner stepped out of the carriage. Each looked over the magnificent structure.

"It's beautiful, Cole, but are you sure that we can afford to stay here—I mean, it looks like it would cost a fortune."

Cole grinned, "I'd say you are about correct. Oh, by the way, we are staying here all right. We are staying here for a week, compliments of Wells Fargo and Company. Consider it part of the reward for stopping that gang of train robbers. Come on, let's get registered. There is a lot to see and do before evening comes."

After registering at the reception desk, Cole received a complimentary copy of *The Daily Morning Call*, San Francisco's most popular newspaper. Cole commented to Laura, "If you want to find out about a town, read its newspaper."

Taking their respective room keys, the couple followed the porter to the second floor. Once again, their rooms were across the hall from each other.

* *

For the next five days, Cole and Laura had the vacation of their dreams. At Cole's suggestion, they looked over the advertisements in the newspaper and selected interesting places to visit.

They rented a hack and driver who drove them on an evening tour of San Francisco. Laura was delighted in observing couples walking the streets, especially the fashions of the ladies. She made plans to shop for herself during their stay.

One evening they took in an opera performance by the renowned Nellie Melba, a famous Australian soprano at the Grand Opera House. Laura found herself mesmerized during the entire performance.

During the day, they toured Chinatown, and found a tasty treat at the Ghirardelli Chocolate Company at Greenwich and Powell Streets. Both Cole and Laura were fascinated by watching the delicious chocolates being made. Free samples proved delectable.

They rode the recently installed cable cars. In fact, they rode them a couple of times. Both were intrigued by the mechanics of the cars, and remarked more than once that San Francisco seemed so modern and forward-thinking.

One afternoon, the couple shared a carriage to The Cliff House, a restaurant atop a hill overlooking the Pacific Ocean. They obtained a basket lunch from the restaurant and picnicked on the lawn overlooking the ocean.

On the final evening before returning to the Lower Colorado, they had dinner in an intimate restaurant along the waterfront. The couple sat at a small table by the window looking directly out over the ocean. The sun resembled a large red ball floating on the horizon at sunset.

Just as twilight descended, a waiter arrived to light a pillar of candles in the center of their table.

Flickering shadows cast the silhouettes on the wall of two people holding hands and gazing into wondrous and longing eyes. Cole was first to speak.

"Laura, I have ridden some long, lonely, and dangerous trails in my life. There were times that I thought that I would never make it. From the first day that I rode on to your ranch, I've held this feeling that we were destined to meet. I looked into your crystal blue eyes and I felt the peace of home for the first time in my adult life. I am proud to have you by my side."

Laura's eyes misted as she smiled the warmest smile that Cole Stockton had ever seen. She wiped her eyes with a handkerchief before speaking. Her voice wavered.

"Cole, I met an older woman back in Texas who foretold of our meeting. I have never forgotten her words. Ever since the first time you looked into my eyes and I read your desire, I have loved you. I carry you in my heart as well as in my mind. I know how you feel about your job as Marshal and I wouldn't have it any other way. I think that we will be together for a long, long time. I am justly proud to be by your side."

The following day they began their return to the Lower Colorado by stagecoach. The trip was a long but a pleasant one. Even so, they were both happy to get back to the beauty and serenity of the Rocky Mountains and the place they called home—Colorado.

* *

Smokey Joe Walker stood at one end of the Denver hotel bar dressed in a fine broadcloth suit with vest and shiny new boots. He sipped a glass of the best whiskey in the house and puffed on a fine cigar.

A small group of young men gathered around him. Each also had a drink and a cigar in his hand. All faces showed excitement as Smokey Joe commenced to tell another of his stories.

"Now then, let me tell you about the time that Cole Stockton and I fought off the Wells Fargo train robbers. Now that was something to behold."

Smokey Joe proudly opened the panel of his coat to reveal the gold colored badge of a Wells Fargo Special Agent on his vest.

CHAPTER TWENTY-ONE

Laura's Dilemma

It had been a year of adventure for Laura Sumner. In the spring, she had finally met her cousin Victoria from back East. Victoria learned what 1878 Colorado was like and she didn't like it at all. By the time she left the Sumner Horse Ranch to return to New York City, both she and Laura knew exactly why Victoria's father had willed the ranch to Laura. Jesse Sumner knew both young women well. His choice of Laura was based upon her strength of character, but most prevalent, her love of horses.

Jesse had observed firsthand Laura's willingness to work with him to learn the multitude of skills necessary to find, corral, and break the wild animals to saddle in order to build her stock. She had the ability to buy and sell that went along with the horse trading business. Victoria, on the other hand, preferred life in the city, fashionable gowns, and keeping company with the social elite.

Next, Laura's parents had faced difficult financial problems. They had almost lost their farm to the greed and corruption of others. Laura along with her closest friend, Cole Stockton, resolved the situation, but only after gunfire.

And then, Laura and Cole had traveled by rail to San Francisco. That journey had turned into another adventure for both. The train had been robbed, causing Cole to delay their West Coast destination. Luckily, Laura's foreman and wranglers could be trusted to run the ranch until she returned.

This eventful year for the Lady from Colorado had passed quickly. Now toward the end of the year in the Lower Colorado, on a frigid day in mid-November, Laura and her wranglers rode the wild foothills to the Rockies in search of wild horses.

By mid-day, good fortune smiled upon them in the form of several sets of hoof prints. The majority of the prints led off to the north.

Two other smaller trails split from the main trail. One led toward the east and the second turned toward the rocky ridges to the northwest. Laura spoke to her foreman, Judd Ellison, "Judd, I'll follow the tracks to the northwest. Please have Eli Johnson track the eastern prints, and the rest of you take on the main trail. I'll meet you back at the ranch toward sundown."

After a long day of hunting wild horses, the wranglers returned to the ranch. Together, they brought several horses to place in the holding corrals next to the barn. The temperature dropped quickly. It had gotten colder and the men were glad to be back to the ranch. The men looked forward to dry clothes, hot coffee, and supper.

Dusk came, and all of the horse hunters had returned. That is, all but Laura, the Boss Wrangler herself. A worried Judd Ellison questioned his men. None had seen or heard from Laura since she waved and rode her black horse, Mickey, out of sight toward the northwest ridges.

When darkness fell, the wranglers became highly concerned. Laura never arrived later than half an hour after sundown. To make matters worse, a severe winter storm was blowing in. Temperatures were sure to drop to below freezing. The wranglers kept a close watch on the weather as they paced nervously back and forth in the barn.

As the moon rose, a wild-eyed Mickey galloped into the ranch yard, reins trailing. The boys knew that Laura would not let Mickey go unless she was in trouble, nor would Mickey leave Laura without good reason.

Winter storms in the Colorado Territory usually brought massive snowfall to the foothills of the Rockies. It would be near impossible to backtrack Mickey at night in such a blizzard. The wranglers knew they would have to wait out the storm. They prayed that Laura was alive and had found shelter from the freezing cold temperatures and furious winds of the storm.

When the wranglers gathered around the potbellied stove in the bunkhouse, their faces reflected the grim situation. United States Marshal Cole Stockton was out on the trail in search of wanted men. Laura was somewhere in the wilds. She was alone, possibly hurt, and surely in need of help. If Laura was to be found, they were the ones to rescue her. What could the seven men do but wait?

As the evening dragged on, the weary wranglers paced the bunkhouse discussing possibilities of where Laura might seek shelter for the night. Would she find a cave? Perhaps she found an abandoned cabin?

The wind howled without mercy for man or beast. An eerie spell fell over the men. Was it Laura's voice crying out in the storm?

Juan Soccorro, a Mexican wrangler and long-time friend of Laura's, moved to the window of the bunkhouse. The glass pane was coated with frozen snow. He went to the door, opened it a crack but saw only the dim light where his wife Emilita was cleaning up the supper dishes. All else was blinding snow flurries. Drifts of snow piled against the ranch buildings.

Judd asked Mike Wilkes and Jeff Sutton to check that the animals in the barn were prepared for the night. They would make sure that all windows and doors were secure. Both men donned their warmest coats and gloves for the task, and stepped out into the icy blast.

Judd and the other wranglers pulled out a handmade map of the foothills. The old foreman considered options for a daybreak search for Laura before he queried, "Boys, where shall we begin at dawn?"

* *

Earlier in the day, Laura had found the tracks of a small bunch of wild horses—about four or five. Excitement had surged through her body. She had wanted to trail this small herd in an attempt to bring them back to the ranch.

The trail led upwards into the perilous lower ridges of the Rockies. Periodically, she lost the trail over rocky ground. Several times she was forced to dismount to study the area. This group had chosen to take to ground higher than most. It was extremely rugged country.

Laura dismounted, walking a distance while leading Mickey. She was so intent studying the trail that she missed seeing the dangerous crevice along the edge of the trail. Without warning, her boots slipped into the narrow space. The young woman immediately felt pain surge through her right leg.

Sharp rock sliced through her Levi's and chaps as she slid into the crevice. A protruding stone tore into the flesh of her right leg. She heard the sudden snap, and knew instantly that her leg was broken.

Laura screamed in pain. Minutes passed as tears rolled down her cheeks. Sweat beads popped along her forehead. She clenched her teeth, caught her breath, and slowly, in agony dislodged herself from the crevice.

Blood soaked her Levi's. The sliver of rock had sliced her leg like a razor. Surely, the break was near the blood.

Laura struggled to stand, but could not. The pain made her weak and dizzy. Again, she attempted to stand, only to stumble and fall hard to the ground. Fear gripped her.

"Mickey!" she cried. "Come here, Mickey."

The black horse moved to her, nuzzling her face as though he could wipe away the sweat and tears. Laura attempted to pull herself up to the stirrup. She was almost erect when yet another stabbing pain wracked through her leg. She fell in a heap beside the stallion.

Laura lay on the cold, hard ground for several minutes. Danger flashed through her mind. She had to climb into the saddle in order to ride to the safety of home. Experience had taught her the perils of this terrain, especially during foul weather.

Once again, she reached up and took hold of a stirrup. She clenched her teeth against the pain in her leg. Her head pounded as she fought the nausea and shock. Slowly, she pulled herself erect on her left leg, leaning against Mickey. She gasped for breath.

Next, Laura grasped the saddle horn in an attempt to hoist herself into the saddle. She was too weak. The pain that shot through her broken leg was unbearable. She feared that she would pass out. She relaxed for a minute against Mickey once more. Her voice was hoarse as she almost whispered, "Must rest a moment."

Laura tried two more times to pull herself up into the saddle. She could not do it. She lost strength after each attempt. Reality hit. Her body rebelled. It was impossible to lift herself, even pull herself, into the saddle. She was weak from fear and pain. She knew that she must send Mickey for help.

Laura breathed heavily as she looked toward the sky. It would be dark soon. She felt the crispness of the air. Dark clouds would bring a drop in temperature. Another winter storm was close at hand. She knew that she must act fast.

Laura leaned against her beloved Mickey. With great effort, she untied the saddle roll and saddlebags, letting them drop to the ground. She managed to lift the canteen and lariat from her saddle and dropped them on the ground, too. Laura pulled the Winchester from the scabbard. She would need all the survival tools that she had with her. Finally, she leaned against Mickey and swallowed hard. Her throat was dry.

"Mickey," she said hoarsely. "Mickey, go home. Mickey, go home to get help."

The black understood, but was reluctant to leave her.

Once again, Laura repeated her instruction to the black horse, "Mickey, go home to get help."

The black horse turned, nuzzled the face of his mistress, then eased away from Laura. She was certain that he understood the urgency of the situation. Mickey trotted off a distance, stopped, and looked back at Laura.

She cried out, "Go, Mickey. Go get help."

The black sprang into a gallop toward the Sumner Ranch.

Laura stood in pain on her good leg until the black stallion galloped out of sight. Then, she slumped to the ground. She lay there gritting her teeth against the pain.

The pain in her leg had taken over her entire body. Even her mind was a blur. "Think, Laura, think hard," she told herself. This woman of strong will knew she must collect her wits to survive the night. She thought, "What to do first? Yes. I must stop the bleeding."

CHAPTER TWENTY-TWO

Salvation

Laura pulled her saddlebags close to open them. With belt knife, she cut and then tore her spare shirt in wide strips. Next, she rolled them for bandages. Looking around, she noticed a few dried limbs lying near the trail. A couple of them looked stout enough for a splint.

Laura dragged herself to them and using her knife stripped two strong branches of all twigs and leaves. These would form a splint to immobilize her right leg. She crawled back to her belongings. She had to rest several times during this relatively short journey, but she never rested very long. The urgency of the situation demanded that she not.

There was just enough water in her canteen to clean the open wound and still leave some for drinking. She took the canteen and gently washed the cuts along her leg. The cold water felt good even though it caused a sting.

The scrapes were superficial. Yet, she was sure they needed more water than she had with her to wash away the dirt and grit. She absolutely must stop this bleeding now. She was tired. Her main concern was the deep gash that continued to bleed profusely.

Laura took a strip of cloth from her roll of bandages, folded it over twice, then placed it over the gash. Next, she applied pressure to it, waiting several minutes before easing up on it. Still, it continued to bleed. She again applied pressure to the wound. The bandage was crimson with blood. The young woman still held pressure to the wound on her leg. Frantically, she grabbed up another strip of shirt cloth from the rolls and added it on top of the first. Finally, she took some strips of cloth and wrapped them snugly around the homemade bandage, tying it in place. The lesser cuts and abrasions would have to wait.

Laura was out of breath. She leaned back to rest a few minutes, considering the pain that she must endure. Her thoughts turned to Cole Stockton. What would Cole do under these circumstances?

Painfully, she reached down to place the two branches along each side of her broken right leg. She wrapped the remaining strips of cloth around her leg and the splints, keeping the cloth as snug as she dared. After that task, she found herself out of breath again and had to rest.

The wind continued to bring icy blasts of night air. She felt chilled. Ironically, sweat poured from her body, soaking her undergarments. Laura knew that she was on the verge of shock. She must gather her survival tools, and find somewhere to crawl to shelter before she passed out.

The young woman gazed around. The sky was dull with heavy overcast. Darkness would bring more wind and surely snow with it. She must find a place out of the wind and out of the snow. She had to find a place where she could build a fire.

On a second sweep of the landscape, she saw it: a crevice among the rocks—twenty yards away. Laura collected her wits and all her strength. She then crawled inch by painful inch to her gear. She reached it, and with very deep breaths, gathered it around herself. Once in reach of it, she studied again the crevice and the terrain in between. Painstakingly, Laura began to inch her way to the crevice—the shelter of life.

Minutes passed quickly as she dragged herself to the crevice. Fear gripped the young woman as gloomy thoughts crossed her mind. Was there enough room in that crevice for her and her gear? Was there room for a fire and fuel? What if there was not room enough? What would she do then?

When Laura reached the dark crevice, she peered cautiously inside. The crevice was deeper than she had judged. There was room enough for one large person as well as all of her survival things. The crevice offered room for a small fire and a pile of fuel.

Laura stuffed her saddle roll, saddlebags, Winchester, and canteen into the crevice. She lay on the ground just outside of the crevice and looked all around the immediate area for tinder and wood to start and keep a fire going.

Old trees yielded an abundance of broken branches and twigs for kindling. Laura crawled slowly around the area to pull up bunches of dried grass and twigs. With a small pile of fuel in the crevice, she took a few minutes to catch her breath before dragging herself back outside to gather larger branches to stockpile.

The wind howled ferociously as she labored. Numb with pain, Laura searched for logs large enough to burn several hours. Finally, she found what she needed.

Looping her lariat around it, she dragged a four-foot length of fallen timber inch by painful inch to the crevice. Exhaustion consumed her aching body. She fought to keep her eyes open. Several times, she found herself nodding to sleep. With sheer determination, she managed to drag the large log into the crevice.

Both snow flurries and the temperature began falling rapidly. Laura lay shivering in the crevice. She closed her eyes and wanted to sleep, but a nagging voice kept her awake.

It was as if Cole Stockton were leaning over her, insisting that she wake up. Laura opened her eyes to learn that she was alone. She was alone, she was hurt, and she was bone chilling cold.

With numbed fingers, she searched her saddlebags and found the matches. She gathered up a clump of dried grass and small twigs. She huddled over the tinder and struck a match, cupping her hands to hide the small flame from the wind.

She placed flame against the small mound of dried grass and twigs. The flame licked hungrily at the fuel and soon a small fire blazed its warming fingers of life. Laura placed some larger pieces of broken tree limbs into the fire. They soon caught and momentarily, she felt the warmth. Her body relaxed a bit.

Slowly, she pulled one end of the four-foot log close to the fire. It would be the next fuel. Flames devoured the large branches that Laura sparingly placed in the fire. She labored to wrestle the larger log into the hungry blaze. The end of the log caught fire. Finally, Laura felt warmth returning to her chilled body.

Laura shivered as she opened her saddle roll and painfully gathered it around her. She tucked her weary sweat and dirt streaked face against her shoulder and hugged herself with her arms. At last, she felt warm.

Laura made herself as comfortable as possible. She reclined against a rock wall in the crevice, and found that she could feed the fire in this position. She took a drink from the canteen.

She thought of food. She could not remember when she had eaten last. Again, she searched her saddlebags. There was beef jerky, cheese, and some cold biscuits along with two apples.

The young woman smiled as she thought, "Cole Stockton lives on this stuff while on the trail. I can do it, too."

Laura bit down on the hard jerky, ripping off a piece with her teeth. As she chewed the tough meat, juices came and it tasted good. She bit into a biscuit. It was hard and crumbly, but nevertheless tasted good. She took another swallow of water.

Now, there was nothing to do but wait. She felt confident that Mickey would go back to the ranch and once her wranglers saw that crucial equipment was missing from Mickey, they would know that she was in trouble. Her men would be out looking for her as soon as they could. Until her wranglers found her, she had to survive on her own.

Laura suddenly recalled her old Uncle Jesse's words, "Sometimes there ain't nothing twix you, God, and the wilds but your own self." She smiled as she remembered Uncle Jesse. He had a saying for almost everything.

Laura dozed off into a deep sleep. She awoke sometime later with the fire low but still giving off heat. She pulled more of the fallen tree into the fire and the flames eagerly feasted on the new portion. Renewed warmth filled the crevice.

It was dark. It was cold. It was windy, and it was snowing hard. Then, she heard them in the distance. It was the long, low, moaning howl of grey wolves, known also as timber wolves. They would be hunting food. Once they caught scent of Laura's blood, they would track her.

Laura shivered as she moved her Winchester closer by. She checked the mechanism and loads. The rifle worked well. Her Colt Lightning revolver with a belt full of cartridges was at the ready. She hoped that they were enough. It was urgent that she now stay awake. Her very life depended on it.

* *

Judd Ellison and the wranglers kept an anxious eye on the intense snowfall while they drank hot black coffee and paced up and down the bunkhouse floor. They had gathered up all the supplies that they would need for a long search. Search routes had been planned, and they had marked areas they would search on the homemade map. They knew all too well the grimness of the situation. Laura Sumner was somewhere out there in a wicked snow storm and she was in trouble.

They had blankets, medical supplies, knives, matches, guns, ammunition, ropes, water, coffee, food, and warm clothes to include heavy winter coats. They also had their own savvy of the trails and lay of the land. They could do no more until the snow stopped.

Throughout the night, the wranglers alternately rested and kept vigil on the weather. Finally, with the gray of early dawn, the snowfall stopped. More than ready to hit the trail, they quickly loaded their rescue supplies to pack horses.

Seven grim-faced men put boot to stirrup and swung up into cold saddles. Foreman Judd Ellison led out toward the northwest foothills of the Rockies.

Each breath produced steam from the men and horses alike. Mickey trotted alongside wrangler Juan Soccorro.

In the back of each man's mind was the constant thought, "We will find Laura and she will be all right." They just had to find her, and quickly.

* *

Laura's body ached all over. Her broken leg throbbed. The deep gash in her leg smarted. She checked the leg, and found it swollen where the break was. That she still had feeling in it was a good sign. Now, she looked to the fire.

The four-foot length of wood was more than half consumed by the fire. It would keep her warm the entire night through as she had fed it sparingly into the flames. She wanted desperately to sleep, but the ever-nagging thought of the wolves kept her mind balanced on the edge of fear and sleep. The throbbing pain in her right leg also helped to keep her awake.

Near to midnight, the snowfall dwindled to only an occasional flurry. The wind died down. The air was still and icy cold. Laura could hear herself breathing. The silence was frightening.

Suddenly, Laura jerked up. She must have dozed. There was a low snarl, and then, she stared straight into the yellow-glazed eyes of a huge timber wolf. His snout was curled up with his fangs bared to her. Thick drool dripped from the wolf's mouth.

Laura cocked the hammer back on the Winchester and raised it slowly. The wolf lunged into the crevice. She pulled the trigger and saw the wolf jerk with the impact of the .44-40 slug. He yelped loudly, but kept snapping at her with ferocious jaws. He was too close for the Winchester.

Laura quickly jerked the Colt Lightning out of her holster and fired pointblank into the animal's face. The wolf immediately slumped to the floor of the crevice.

More wolves squirmed to the crevice entrance. Each snarled loudly. They grabbed the fallen wolf with their fangs and dragged the carcass out of the crevice. The pack fought over their fallen brother and ripped its body to pieces.

Laura lay back trembling with fear as she held the Winchester pointed at the entrance to the crevice. Another wolf attempted to slide into the opening. She fired into him. The wolf yelped and backed out. The pack likewise attacked the wounded wolf.

Then there was silence. Laura peered out of the crevice with red-rimmed, weary eyes. She saw the wolves cautiously circling around the opening of the crevice. They would wait her out. She had to sleep sometime, and then they would have her.

Laura thought hard—she had to stay awake. How could she? She thought of Cole Stockton. She thought of his arms around her. How warm they would be. She thought of his eyes. She always felt warm and comfortable when he looked at her. She felt the warmth of his soul reaching out to her, and gently stoking the passion of her feelings. She could almost feel the touch of his hand on her cheek. She wished that he were here with her.

The wolves came closer. She fired another round.

* *

Judd Ellison and the wranglers reached an area that they figured Laura had to have ridden over. They split up and fanned out across the area, riding roughly a quarter of a mile apart from one another. Their eyes eagerly searched the snow-covered landscape. What were they looking for? They were looking for anything that seemed out of the ordinary.

Minutes wore on and turned into hours. Half a day passed and yet, no sign of Laura. The men halted for a quick fire and coffee. They huddled together around the small fire and tried to think like Laura. What would Laura be doing? She would be looking for wild horses or trails left by them. She would have followed them.

"Alright," called out Judd to the wranglers. "Keep looking for signs of Laura, but also look for sign of horses. If we find signs of horses, we may find Laura." The others nodded agreement.

The men mounted and fanned out again, working further toward the ridges to the northwest. Two more hours passed when the faint sound of gunfire in the distance caught their attention. They pulled up short to listen. No one moved or spoke for some time as they waited.

Suddenly, a distinct shot filled the air. Then, another shot, and another, and another. There were several more shots in succession. Then, there was silence.

The wranglers got their bearings, and then spurred their mounts toward the direction of the gunfire. A lump came to each man's throat as they steadily worked their way through the snow.

* *

The fire had now consumed all of the four-foot log and was dying down. Laura began shivering with the icy cold. More wolves were inching forward. The wolves sensed her fear and began to close in on her. Laura was worn down, and they were ready.

The pack would harass her until her ammunition was gone. They could smell the blood of her wounds and they wanted it. They were braver now, coming closer. Laura was blurry-eyed from lack of sleep, a weakening of her stamina, and pain wracked from her broken and cut leg.

Laura fired her Winchester out of the crevice until it was empty. She fired her Colt until it was empty. The exhausted woman could no longer control her shaking hands. Through sheer will power, she somehow reloaded and fired again, and again, and again.

The crevice filled with the odor of gunsmoke. Her eyes burned from the acid smoke and lack of sleep. Tears filled her eyes and blurred her vision. She faced a menacing painful death.

Laura pointed the Colt Lightning at the wolf that suddenly appeared at the entrance to the crevice. She squeezed the trigger. A metallic click told her that the revolver was empty for the last time. There was no more ammunition.

She grabbed up a smoldering stick from the fire and held it in front of her. Fire was her last defense.

Suddenly, shots rang out. A multitude of shots reverberated through the crisp air. Rifles fired repeatedly. The wolf lunged forward into the crevice.

Laura jammed the fiery stick into the wolf's open jaws with all the strength that she could muster. She fumbled around for the belt knife. She grabbed it in her hand. The wolf was impaled on the firebrand and she stabbed it as hard as her strength allowed.

Long minutes ticked by before the dead wolf was jerked from the crevice. Laura lay back gasping for breath. Moments later, she looked up into the red-rimmed, but relief-filled eyes of Judd Ellison. Tears of relief streamed down her dirty face. Her wranglers had found her.

Within minutes, her boys had her out of the crevice, and alongside a blazing fire. They wrapped her in heavy blankets. They had coffee boiling. Mike Wilkes and Juan Soccorro examined her leg. Juan broke open the medical kit and tended to her leg.

Juan cleaned and dressed the cuts. He reset her leg with a fresh splint. Laura was tenderly cared for. She was fed a hastily prepared hot broth from the shavings of beef jerky, as well a tin cup of hot coffee to warm her.

While Juan worked to ease Laura's pain, several wranglers set to work to gather the pelts of the wolves. The pelts of wolves in horse and cattle country brought generous bounties, not to mention that they made extremely warm gloves and winter hats.

When Laura acknowledged that she was ready to travel, her men placed her gently on a travois, and bundled her up for the trip home. Mickey nuzzled her face, and she smiled as she stroked his forehead.

The trip home seemed extra long and bumpy, but Laura didn't it mind a bit. She was safe with her wranglers. She had endured under great odds and survived. She was a woman of the West.

* *

Two days later, a trail weary U. S. Marshal Cole Stockton dismounted in front of the Sumner Ranch stables and led Warrior to his stall. He took note of the ten wolf pelts nailed along the outer wall of the stable and wondered about them.

"Must have had some wolf trouble," he muttered to himself.

Cole crossed the ranch yard and entered the house to find Laura wrapped in her robe and reclining on the sofa in front of the fireplace.

Her right leg was in a splint and lay propped on a pillow. She smiled with a radiance known only to him.

"What happened to your leg?" he asked.

"It's a long story, Cole. Put another log on the fire and come here. I've missed you so very much."

Cole Stockton knelt beside the sofa and leaned toward Laura.

Their eyes met with yearning. He leaned closer to her. Their lips met in a smoldering kiss as their arms embraced one another. Laura was alive with vibrant beauty and he whispered such into her ear as she snuggled closer to him. All was right with the world, and with *The Lady from Colorado.*

Printed in the United States
By Bookmasters